"Maybe we should rehearse our role as a couple," he clarified.

In New York, she deflected men as easily as breathing, a prickly vibe built into everything about her appearance and manner. But the skill eluded her with Chase, as if her body refused to transmit the "don't touch" signals she sent to everyone else.

"Are you regarding this as rehearsal?" she finally managed to say, glancing down at his wandering hand. "Because I'm not sure winding me up is the same thing as making me feel comfortable around you."

"I look forward to hearing all about the difference after we get settled." His voice smoked along her senses before he eased back.

Then, opening the driver's side door, he exited the vehicle, leaving her hot and bothered as well as confused. She hated not knowing his endgame for this engagement, but she couldn't deny that being around him again aroused her.

That was dangerous for her peace of mind.

* * *

The Stakes of Faking It by Joanne Rock is part of the Brooklyn Nights series.

Dear Reader,

Has there ever been a time when you wanted to escape your life? My heroine, Tana, ran hard from her family's shady past to shape a new life for herself in New York City as an actress. She's made new friends and even has a leading role in a small play. But when her past comes calling in the form of rancher Chase Serrano, her carefully reimagined future is threatened.

Chase has never forgotten the woman who vanished from his Nevada ranch and left him wondering if anything they'd shared had been real. He needs her help now, and considering her role in her father's con to steal his inheritance, he won't take no for an answer. If only he wasn't as attracted to her as ever!

I hope you enjoy Tana's story. I've had so much fun writing the heroines of the Brooklyn Nights series. I'll be sorry to leave the brownstone and the friendships that kept me smiling as I worked!

Happy reading,

Joanne Rock

JOANNE ROCK

THE STAKES OF FAKING IT

HARLEQUIN
DESIRE

ISBN-13: 978-1-335-73525-6

The Stakes of Faking It

Harlequin Enterprises ULC
22 Adelaide St. West, 40th Floor
Toronto, Ontario M5H 4E3, Canada
www.Harlequin.com

Printed in U.S.A.

Joanne Rock credits her decision to write romance after a book she picked up during a flight delay engrossed her so thoroughly that she didn't mind at all when her flight was delayed two more times. Giving her readers the chance to escape into another world has motivated her to write over eighty books for a variety of Harlequin series.

Visit her Author Profile page at Harlequin.com, or joannerock.com, for more titles.

You can also find Joanne Rock on Facebook, along with other Harlequin Desire authors, at Facebook.com/harlequindesireauthors!

For the dreamers. I'm rooting for you!

One

The outdoor audience in Brooklyn Bridge Park held its collective breath as the last scene in the *A Streetcar Named Desire* reboot rolled to its inevitable conclusion. Tana Blackstone was playing against type in her role as Blanche DuBois, even in this version's younger and grittier twenty-first-century retelling. But that didn't stop her from nailing her final line as the doomed femme fatale.

"I've always depended on the kindness of strangers." Tana batted her lashes at the actor playing the doctor character whose job it was to cart poor Blanche off to a psychiatric hospital.

Wrapping her hand around the actor's arm, Tana walked off stage right with him while the other players concluded the scene. The production had been months in the making in the small temporary venue, as they'd waited for the pandemic to ease enough that audiences would come out for performances.

Tana had been lucky to be tapped for this one considering her limited professional résumé. But too many other talented actresses had either left the city or taken alternate work during the Broadway shutdown. She'd been close to having to bail out of the profession when this job offer arrived.

"Brava," her colleague, an older man with shaggy white eyebrows and a grizzled beard, whispered to her a moment later as the audience burst into thunderous applause. "Well done, Tana."

"Thanks." She tugged on the short, tight skirt her part called for since this version of Blanche was a burned-out club kid with a predilection for prescription painkillers. "It was a fun show."

They pivoted to take their curtain calls for their small but appreciative outdoor audience. The show wasn't Broadway quality, but it'd been well directed, and the fans had obviously missed theater as much as the actors had during the pandemic.

Waiting her turn to take her bows, Tana cheered for the rest of the cast. She was so new to the city that she'd never had the chance to even try out for a Broadway show, so she couldn't "miss it" exactly. Still, she would have liked to see how she'd fare in a big audition.

She might have gotten her performing experience unconventionally as the offspring of professional grifters, but she'd been acting for as long as she could remember. At five years old, she pranced around wealthy neighborhoods with stray dogs her father cleaned up to sell as pedigreed pooches. Tana had cried her eyes out every time she lost one of her temporary "pets" to the scheme, but she'd learned to identify kindness in potential pet families really quickly so at least she'd consoled herself that the animals were going to better homes. By the age of ten, she could have won Tony Awards for her recurring role of "lost girl" so her mother could pickpocket people who stopped to help, another job she'd resented bitterly, but her parents had threatened to put her into foster care if she didn't comply. She'd been just frightened enough of the possibility to wade through another demoralizing day.

The moment she turned eighteen, she'd told her dad she was done with cons and using her acting skills for his personal gain. If only she'd escaped the life a little sooner than that last summer between high school and college. Instead, she'd unwittingly tangled herself in the middle of one of her dad's biggest scams while doing nothing more than living under his roof. In the end, her father had swindled a widow out of her ranchlands at the same time the widow's son stole Tana's heart.

These days, she confined her performances to the theater. As she stepped downstage to take her bows for her role as Blanche, she told herself that she was finally where she belonged. The theater world was her new family. The outdoor audience full of young families seated on picnic blankets with strollers in tow paid her for her work because they wanted to see her act, not because they were getting separated from their wallets by sleight of hand. Finally, she had something to offer others rather than just taking. A few whistles and calls of "brava!" made her heart smile.

Lifting her fingers to her lips, she blew kisses into the crowd, soaking up their joy for a few more seconds as her gaze roved the groups of people breaking up on the lawn. Then her eye stuttered to a stop on a man standing alone in the center of the lower orchestra seats—aka, the stretch of grass between the front of the stage and a bicycle path.

He was a tall, athletic figure dressed in dark jeans and vintage T-shirt, a black jacket hugging broad shoulders as he put a Stetson back on his head. The man's mahogany-colored hair and olive skin made the women around him look twice. Or maybe it was his pale gray eyes, or the dark shadow along the sculpted jaw.

Her knees turned to water at the sight of him, but not because he was an outrageously good-looking man.

No. She felt faint because Chase Serrano was a ghost from the past she thought she'd never face again.

"Tana!" one of her coactors whispered from behind, pulling Tana from her musing, reminding her she was hogging the spotlight, albeit unwittingly.

Whoops.

Heart pounding wildly, she scuttled off the stage,

brain working overtime to puzzle out what just happened. Deaf to the atmosphere of happy celebration around her, she wound her way through clusters of colleagues toward a trailer parked behind the stage. She needed to get out of here, away from the apparition she'd just seen in the audience.

Because how could it possibly be Chase Serrano, the very same rancher who'd once captured her heart? The one whose widowed mom lost his inheritance by signing it over to con man Joe Blackstone? Tana's dear old dad.

She raced down the steps that led away from the staging area, then jogged to the cramped trailer where the female cast members could dress and store their bags during the performances. The security guard, a tall former roller derby queen, nodded to Tana before opening the door to admit her.

"I hope you're not going to take off before we go out for drinks," Lorraine said, peering into the dimly lit trailer while Tana riffled through a stack of sweaters and lightweight jackets to find her satchel.

"I can't tonight." Tana pulled off her jet-black wig, then yanked the ponytail holder from her own brown hair that had been hidden beneath. The ends were normally dyed pink, but she noticed the cotton-candy color was fading as she ran her fingers through the strands. "Sorry, Lorraine. Maybe next time."

She checked her appearance one last time in the mirror. Not that she was trying to look good. If anything, she hoped her altered appearance would ensure she wouldn't be recognized if that had really been Chase in the audience. Yanking a wipe out of a packet in her purse, she scrubbed the towelette over her face to remove a layer of stage makeup, all the while wondering how Chase had found her.

And even more concerning, what could he possibly want with her? She'd already left Nevada to begin her arts degree in a small town north of New York City by the time Chase's mom married her dad and all hell broke loose on the ranch. She'd assumed Chase had been in Idaho where he would have been starting his finance program. But he could have been living most anywhere when he sent her that final cruel text accusing her of being part of the con and using her virginity as "misdirection," so Chase missed the signs of what was happening with his mom.

"You don't need to be sorry, sweetie," Lorraine said, her New Jersey accent coming through. "I'll still be having myself a fine time." She polished her long red fingernails on her T-shirt, chuckling softly. "Tonight's the night I make a move on Stella."

Megan, the actress who played Tana's sister in the play, was one of the sweetest cast members, but she had about as much discernment in partners as Stella Kowalski.

"Really?" Shimmying off her skirt, Tana peered out the trailer's only window, looking for the man she thought she'd seen. But there were no signs of a Stetson anywhere. "Good luck. If Megan's smart, she'll see that you're worth ten of the players she's been dating."

She let go of the window blind and pulled on her denim cutoffs, not even bothering to layer the leggings she would have normally worn underneath.

Time was of the essence.

Heading toward the door again, she paused at Lorraine's narrow-eyed look where the other woman still leaned into the Airstream.

"Is everything okay?" Lorraine asked, scrutinizing Tana's face. "You look like a woman with trouble on her heels."

"Just hoping to avoid someone from the audience," Tana admitted, more concerned with a speedy exit than protecting her secret. "If anyone asks for me—I don't care if it's Scorsese himself—I'd be grateful if you say you don't know anything, okay?"

Frowning, Lorraine leaned back to give her room to pass. "Sure thing, honey. I can get someone to escort you to the train station—"

Tana was already rushing by her, head swiveling as she searched the crowd on Pier One for signs of the black jacket and mahogany-colored hair beneath the rim of a cowboy hat. "Thanks. And I'll be fine. See you Wednesday."

She berated herself for not bringing a hat today as she hitched her satchel higher on her shoulder and navigated the pedestrian traffic at an inconspicuous pace. There'd been a time in her life when she wouldn't have left the house without a slouchy, wide-brimmed hat in her backpack, but she hadn't needed to blend into the background for a long time. Still, the old tricks returned now. Stick to the middle of a group. Don't move too quickly. Head down.

She was just debating whether or not to drop down into the closest subway station when a familiar voice spoke next to her ear.

"Hello, Hustler."

Her stomach sank.

She should have kept walking. Instead, she stopped short as abruptly as if he'd lassoed her the way he used to do with running calves. She stumbled just enough to make the man beside her catch her elbow in one strong hand.

Too late to run now. Tana had no choice but to brazen it out. Steeling herself, she looked up into the light gray eyes of the only man she'd ever bared her soul to.

A man she'd lived to bitterly regret.

"Hello, Chase."

Chase Serrano willed himself to loosen his grip on Tana Thorpe. No. Make that Tana Blackstone. He should have gotten used to the fact that he'd known her by an alias all those years ago.

Everything about her had been a lie.

She'd been an artful creation of male fantasy, from her wide-eyed interest in ranch life to her breathless admission of virginity. And while that last bit had technically been true, a discovery he'd made the night of her eighteenth birthday, Chase had to assume her innocence had been calculatingly bestowed where it would do the most good for her family's confidence games.

He'd done all the research he could on Joe Blackstone and his family once he'd learned the true identity of "Joe Thorpe." The man had married his mother and promptly sold off the family ranch that had been in Chase's mother's name at the time. The Blackstone patriarch was creative in his scams, sometimes involving his daughter, Tana, and his then-legal wife, Alicia, Tana's absentee mother who'd since divorced him. Joe had been married at least three other times under false names.

Had Tana continued the family business?

Chase released her slender arm. He didn't think he could stop glaring at her, however. There was simply no other way to look at a woman who'd helped swindle him out of his birthright. Around them, dozens of park-goers headed toward the subway station as twilight fell, while bicyclists and runners darted by. A few dog walkers, their pets sporting light-up leashes and collars.

Despite the bustle, Chase's world had narrowed to the thief in front of him. She was petite and delicately made, her features so fine they looked like they belonged on a fairy-tale princess. She had high cheekbones, full, rosy lips and chocolate-brown eyes. She looked different now with the bright pink ends on the glossy brown waves he remembered from eight years ago, however. There were new tattoos on her wrists and a diamond stud winking on one side of her nose, too. Even her clothes were a far cry from the simple T-shirts and jeans she'd favored that long-ago summer. Now she wore cutoffs with a heavy belt covered in spikes that hugged narrow hips. A pair of black combat boots were so scuffed he wondered if they'd actually seen combat. Her white T-shirt had a graphic of a spider on a dizzying Escher-like background. He knew the wild outfit wasn't part of the show she'd just been in, because he'd watched the whole thing.

And he hadn't been the least bit surprised that she was a talented actress. She'd been playing a role every second they'd spent together.

Too bad the anger he still harbored about that didn't keep him from noticing this woman was still undeniably appealing.

Damn it.

"We need to talk." He pointed in the direction of One Hotel, on the opposite end of Pier One from where they were standing. "My hotel is over there."

Her eyebrow lifted. "No hotels on the first date, thanks. How did you find me?"

"Does it matter?" He refused to let her commandeer this conversation. He'd done the legwork to find her, and he wasn't leaving until she'd committed to his plan. "If you don't mind discussing your criminal past in the middle of a public park, that's fine. But we'd have more privacy if we sat in a quiet corner of the hotel's rooftop lounge."

Her cheeks flushed briefly at his words, but she still gave him a tight smile.

"There's nothing you can say to me that can't be

said on a park bench." She thumbed to the right, indicating a vacant spot under the trees. "I can give you five minutes before I need to leave for my next appointment."

Without waiting for his answer, she marched toward the bench. The park lights were on now, illuminating the ground around the base of the tree, but the seating area itself remained dim. Swinging her satchel to the ground, Tana dropped onto the wooden slats and crossed her legs before hooking her hands around one knee. She looked at him expectantly.

This wasn't exactly the way he'd envisioned this interview playing out, but so be it. She wanted to talk in a park, then he would lay it all on the line right here.

"You're going to help me." He lowered himself onto the bench beside her.

"How kind of me." She looked up into the tree overhead as if lost in thought while she listened.

He wondered briefly if she avoided looking at him for another reason. Did she not want to face the past? Or could she feel any remorse about what she'd done?

"We both know you owe me more than you can ever repay, so I want to make it clear I'm not asking for your help. I'm demanding it."

That got her attention. Her brown eyes flickered over him.

"I don't know where my father is anymore, so if that's what you want to know, you're bound to be disappointed. My mother couldn't even find him to notify him of their divorce."

"That's not what I'm here for." Although he found it interesting she assumed he cared about that. Did she know that he'd regained Cloverfield Ranch? Remade his father's fortune twice over? "The police will deal with him if he ever resurfaces."

"How's your mom?" she asked suddenly, nibbling the corner of her lip as if she wanted to take the question back.

"Better off without your father in her life," he informed her coldly. "I moved her out of Nevada immediately after her fake husband disappeared so she wouldn't be surrounded by bad memories of her phony family."

Tana's lashes lowered at the jab. Not that he thought her capable of shame. But he hadn't intended to make this meeting an airing of grievances. Tana Blackstone's day of reckoning wouldn't be about that. She might have escaped legal charges in the hustle that stole his inheritance, since she'd been the one to notify the police about her dad using a fake name while living in Nevada. And from a police perspective, she hadn't materially participated in the land scam.

But that didn't mean she was not guilty.

"Good." Her soft answer was almost lost in the shrill whistle of a bicyclist on a nearby path.

A small dog off the leash darted out of the cyclist's way, the harried owner running behind.

Chase remembered well the feeling of never catching up. Thankfully, those days were almost behind him now. Reclaiming his father's fortune had gone a long way toward soothing some of the fury the Blackstones had left in their wake.

Now he just needed one last missing piece to restore his birthright.

"I know you're under a time constraint, so I'll come right to the point."

She shifted to face him more fully. Alert. Curious.

He continued, glad for the excuse to be as succinct as possible. The quicker she agreed to his terms, the better. "I've spent the better part of the last eight years recovering what your father stole from my family. The money, of course. But more importantly—to me—the land."

"You were able to buy back Cloverfield?" Tana's brown eyes widened as she toyed with a heavy silver bangle on her wrist.

The gesture reminded him of the way she'd played her character on stage, the nervous gestures that had made Blanche DuBois seem so fragile. Did Tana think she could pretend to be anyone other than the coldhearted con he knew her to be?

"Offering far more than it was worth helped my cause," he said drily, failing to keep the old bitterness in check. "I thought the score was settled once I reclaimed the ranch."

"But that's not enough for you." She leaned against the back of the bench, but still eyed him warily.

Behind her, the lights of Manhattan on the other side of the East River made a bright backdrop.

"It might have been enough, if the parcel of land

had been the same one my father meant for me to have once I turned twenty-one."

Her forehead wrinkled as she scrunched her nose. The diamond stud refracted the light, twinkling in the growing darkness. "I don't understand. I thought my dad sold the whole thing to a horse breeder from Tennessee?"

"I did, too. I was so confident of that, I allowed an agent to handle the deal for me." Chase had been overseas on business, preferring to avoid his old hometown full of bad memories. He had an ongoing dispute with a powerful neighbor who'd taken advantage of the upheaval in the Serrano household that summer. Another score he still needed to settle. "It wasn't until I visited the property myself last winter that I realized a small portion of the original parcel was not included in the sale."

"I don't understand. Why would he sell most of the ranch but not all of it? Who has the rest?"

He studied her now, from the cadence of her voice to the expression in her eyes, looking for a tell that would betray her. He'd read a lot about swindles and the con artists who pulled them, educating himself on how he'd been screwed out of his fortune. But despite his studies, he couldn't spot any hint that she already knew what he was about to tell her.

"That's the amusing part of all this," Chase pressed on. "It turns out the land has been held in trust for you."

A beat of silence followed his news.

"That's impossible." She shivered slightly and

wrapped her arms around herself. "I assure you, I don't own any land. Not in Nevada, and not anywhere else. Look at the tax rolls and see for yourself."

"It's been controlled by a trust for the last eight years. They've paid the taxes consistently." It had taken him months to hunt down the information since the title currently belonged to a shell company.

Technically, he probably shouldn't have been able to trace the trust back to her, because those holding companies were well paid for their discretion. But he'd spared no expense to obtain the proof he required.

She shook her head and held out her arms, shrugging her shoulders. "Do you really think I'd be living on ramen noodles and popcorn in this most expensive of all cities if I could have sold off some mystery piece of property for income? I'm still paying back loans to a state school, Chase."

He had researched enough to know this was true. But then, he wasn't so naive as to believe the daughter of a successful con man didn't know a thing or two about hiding what she didn't want other people to see.

"I assure you, the trust is for you. I don't know why you haven't been contacted by them if you were really unaware of this, but it's yours to claim legally at any time."

"Great. If you care to share the contact information, I'll go cash in. Obviously, the land is yours in the first place, so I'll sign it over to you." She reached for her satchel and passed him a card with her contact information. Then she made a move to stand. "I really do need to go—"

After shoving her card in his pocket, he rested a hand on her knee. He'd just meant to catch her attention so she stayed put, but the momentary brush of her bare thigh under his palm was enough to send sparks through him.

"Wait. That's not all." He let go of her again, noting the way she covered the spot he'd touched with one hand. "I need you to go to Nevada with me to sort out the paperwork."

"Why?" Frowning, she shook her head. "You just told me you had an agent buy your land for you. Why do I need to go in person for this?"

"This is more complicated." Which was the truth. But he had other reasons for wanting her to return to his hometown with him. Plans far bigger than he was ready to share today.

"I can't leave New York. I have a life here. I'm doing a show—"

"First of all, I've already checked the performance schedule, and you don't have a show at the time I need your help. And second, you owe me." He let the weight of that reminder settle around her narrow shoulders. "You and your father robbed my mother, Tana. There's no other word for it."

"That's not true." She chewed a fingernail for a second before ripping it away from her mouth. "I didn't rob anyone. I just had the misfortune of still living under my father's roof that summer."

"A misfortune for us both, then," he reminded her

softly, not letting her off the hook. "Since you served as my distraction while your father took everything my mom owned."

She pursed her lips and took a moment before answering, her brown eyes shooting daggers.

"For the record, my purpose was never to distract you. And assuming I can take the time off for a trip, when would I need to go?" She shouldered her bag and stood.

He rose, too, keeping his tone conversational. Easy.

Preparing her for the bigger request.

"This weekend. We need to fly out on Friday evening."

"As in three days from now?"

He nodded. "Yes. Your play isn't running thanks to the book festival on the pier."

He'd done his homework, and he wouldn't let her off the hook.

"I don't understand—"

"I didn't understand when you disappeared from my life forever, either. But that didn't change the fact."

Hesitating, she looked away from him, as if scanning the horizon might provide answers. Then, she nodded.

"Fine. I'll make it work." She tucked a few strands of brown and pink hair behind one ear, her feet already shuffling in place as if she couldn't wait to sprint away. "Just message me the details and I can meet you at the airport."

Relieved, he felt one of the knots in his chest un-kink a bit. He needed her help, and he'd known going into this meeting that she could very well refuse him.

"I know where you live. I'll send a car. But Tana?" His heart thudded at the knowledge that he was so close to recovering his family legacy.

Close to having the vengeance he craved on the Blackstones.

"Yes?" Impatience threaded through her voice and body language, shoulders stiff and feet shifting.

Maybe it was wrong to take pleasure from her discomfort. But he'd lost too much at her hands to care. If anything, he savored the moment to extract one last thing.

"You'll be traveling as my fiancée."

Two

A stress headache pounded behind Tana's right eye. She felt her heartbeat pulse there, causing a tic. Normally, she was skilled at hiding her emotions and showing the world only what she wanted them to see. But an encounter with Chase Serrano blew that all to hell and back.

Bad enough he'd sought her out in the first place after eight years of believing the worst about her. But now she knew he'd been investigating her background, making himself familiar with her life and— no doubt—her lack of accomplishments in the years she'd been struggling to find direction. He wanted to drag her back to the setting of their affair where she'd experienced gut-wrenching betrayals.

Her father had conned the family of the guy she'd

fallen for. The guy she'd fallen for blamed her for it all. Then her mother had washed her hands of the whole thing, choosing to divorce Joe Blackstone in absentia while telling Tana she'd rather not associate with anyone who would narc on her own father.

Why on earth would Chase want to go back to the site of the implosion while she wore his ring? As if their relationship wasn't colossally screwed-up enough.

"You can't be serious." She jammed her fingers into her hair near her scalp, massaging the front of her head in an effort to relieve the thumping pressure.

It wasn't fair that he looked so good while taking a wrecking ball to her carefully constructed life. His broad shoulders blocked her view of Manhattan. All she could see was the vee of his chest tapering to narrow hips. Muscular thighs hugged by dark denim.

Realizing she was staring, she tipped her chin up again, only to catch him smirking, well aware of where her gaze had drifted.

"Quite serious. It's a nonnegotiable point." He checked the oversize watch on one wrist, the rose-gold face glinting briefly in the landscape lights where she spotted the Patek Philippe name below the date. "Can I walk you where you need to go next? I don't want to detain you further."

"How kind of you," she drawled, glancing around the pier at the evening crowd. She didn't need a babysitter to walk her own neighborhood, but she also wanted to be home as quickly as possible after this craptastic day. "I'm going this way."

Grateful to be moving so she could work off some of the nervous energy from this encounter, Tana led him up Furman Street toward Old Fulton. They walked in silence so long that she wondered what his game was.

"Don't you think you owe your would-be fiancée some explanation for this bizarre request?" she asked finally, keeping her focus on the sidewalk. Pedestrian traffic was lighter away from the park, but she was grateful for any distraction from Chase's probing gray eyes. "Why on earth would you want to fake an engagement with me?"

Even as the words tumbled from her mouth, however, a possible explanation rose to top of her mind. She halted under the trees of Cadman Plaza Park, near the stone steps to one of the entrances.

"What?" he asked, halting a step ahead of her and turning to read her expression.

"Don't tell me you think a public engagement will bring my father out of hiding." She spun the ring on her thumb, agitated and restless.

Joe Blackstone had fled the country eight years ago, and she hadn't heard from him since. A couple of times, blank postcards had arrived from exotic locales with no signatures, just strings of numbers that meant nothing to her. She knew they were from him.

Even that had ended once she finished her stint at college.

But he hadn't called. Hadn't emailed. Hadn't written.

"Probably not," Chase admitted slowly. "But if

nothing else, your dad will hear about it." His voice turned low and gritty. "He'll know I've taken back what he stole from me."

For the briefest moment, she saw past the anger in Chase's eyes to the hurt of betrayal. But then he turned on his heel and continued walking.

Which was strange, since he'd volunteered to accompany *her*. But oh well. She followed him since he was going the direction she was headed anyhow. Her chest ached with the memories of the way her father had sold Chase's family lands right out from under him. It had happened too fast, while she'd been away at her student orientation in the small-town college outside New York City. By the time she learned of his betrayal, her dad was long gone.

She had no way of taking out her fury on him for hurting someone she loved. Of course, that relationship had taken a nosedive immediately afterward, with Chase convinced she'd been in on the con.

She'd tried to warn him, hadn't she? She'd advised him ahead of time that her father was not to be trusted. But since she could only guess what her dad might do, she hadn't been able to be specific about what to watch out for. Especially when her parents' old threats of foster care had morphed into threats of sending her to juvie for the role Tana had played in their past schemes. She'd just wanted to hang on until she turned eighteen and went to college, where she could finally have some freedom and a safe place to live far away from them. Her head throbbed harder, and she squeezed both temples at the same time.

"I can't believe you're doing this," she murmured, mostly to herself, as they neared the Korean War Veterans Plaza.

"Your father likes games. He'll appreciate this one." The steel threading through his tone made her glance over at him.

His jaw flexed as he stared straight ahead. Even so, he pulled her against him when a reckless bicyclist whizzed past on the sidewalk where he did not belong.

Momentarily squeezed to his side, Tana relived a hundred memories of being in this man's arms in an instant. She inhaled the woodsy and musky scent that catapulted her back to his truck bed in the moonlight, a bonfire just outside the open tailgate. His warm palm curved around her hip recalled the way he'd steered her where he wanted her that first unforgettable time together. She'd visited him in the barn he'd been converting to a bunkhouse, and somehow they'd ended up tangled together...

She straightened away from him, cheeks hot. The memories of her happiness were too much to take right now. She'd left that person and that life far behind. Better to focus on the present. And his frustrating reasons for a fake engagement.

"So this is all a game to you?" With a tug on her shirt, she resumed their brisk pace. She still felt off-stride, however, and knew it had everything to do with Chase's presence beside her.

"You and your father made my life a game." He stopped as they reached a crosswalk, then turned to face her. His gray eyes were serious under the light of the streetlamp. "And I won't forget that."

She swallowed past the lump in her throat that was all guilt, even though she hadn't been the one to set Chase up. She should have known her father was making a big score, but she hadn't been part of the scam since she'd chosen to be done with that life. At the time, she'd believed her father was just trying to convince widow Margot Serrano to invest in some bogus business. She'd warned Chase about that, in fact, telling him to watch out for his mother's finances on the pretense that she didn't trust her dad's financial savvy.

Little did she know her father had his eye on a bigger prize, eloping with Margot after Tana left for school, and selling the ranch as part of their plan to "travel the world." Except then her dad emptied their joint bank account and got a flight for himself in secret, leaving Chase's mother waiting for him at the airport, her bags packed for a Paris trip that never happened. Or so she'd gleaned from the news coverage of the police report on the crime when Chase brought the cops into the case. She'd understood then why Chase hadn't returned her calls. Understood he must hate her.

Especially when she'd received one last ugly text from him, accusing her of using seduction to distract him from what was happening between his mother and her dad. They'd never spoken again until today.

"It was never a game for me," she said finally, knowing he wouldn't believe her but needing to put it out there. "I don't blame you for hating me for what my father stole, but I had no idea what he was planning since I told him I'd report him to the authorities the moment I turned eighteen. He kept me in the dark those last few months."

He held her gaze for a moment longer, then gave a rueful shake of his head, a bitter smile playing about his lips.

"So you say." He crossed the street, hastening his pace. After a moment, he glanced back at her. "Are you headed back to your place?"

She missed a step. Then rushed to keep up with him. "I forgot that you already mentioned you know where I live."

"Yes. You didn't think I just accidentally happened to find you at your performance in the park today, did you?" He shoved his hands in his jacket pockets, slowing down to wait for her. "I looked you up when I discovered you owned a piece of Cloverfield."

It wouldn't have been difficult to locate her, even without a private eye. Her name had been in some prominent New York news outlets when she'd won a coveted spot in her Brooklyn brownstone, a sponsored residence for women seeking careers in artistic professions. Tana had submitted a clip of her acting, but she'd since discovered a love for the production end, as well.

As they passed Brooklyn Borough Hall, they traversed a wide pedestrian path lined on either side with trees and old-fashioned streetlamps that cast a golden glow on the late-summer evening.

"Have you been in New York long?" she asked, wondering exactly how much he knew about her.

"In the city? No. But I bought a house in the Hamptons last year, so I've spent a few months there."

She did a double take, trying to picture the man she'd once known mingling with the East Coast elite. "The Hamptons? Since when do cowboys take homes in towns known for their social cachet filled with beautiful people?"

"Since I had to earn back a small fortune to regain my father's legacy. You recall I was studying finance in school?" At her nod, he continued, "I parlayed that into investing. Access to some of the country's wealthiest families has been good for business."

"But…the Hamptons?" She recalled the weeks she'd spent with him on the ranch when they'd spent hours riding. "It's hard for me to picture you spending a day where you're not on the back of a horse."

She peered up at him in his dark Stetson, the hat shadowing his clear gray eyes. Their gazes met for a moment, memories flooding back of those long trips they'd taken into the mountains. He'd shown her the things he loved about the dramatic Humboldt Range in northern Nevada, and she'd fallen for both the man and the place. She looked away first, clearing her dry throat.

"I purchased a house with stables," he admitted a moment later, pulling her gaze back to him. "But

I bought the property as an investment, as well. I'll keep it until I can turn a nice profit on a sale."

They walked in silence a little longer, crossing onto Fulton Street before he spoke again. "What about you? Are you going to tell me what you're really doing in New York?"

"What do you mean? You know what I'm doing. I'm acting in a play and trying to build a career. The same as I've always wanted." Except now she also wanted to work behind a camera, too.

"Come on. We both know that's not true."

She stiffened at his tone, the bitterness returning as they passed a food cart selling halal food, the scents of coriander and cumin tingeing the air.

"I assure you it is. But since you're anxious to remind me that I'm not a good person, why don't you tell me what you think I'm doing in New York?"

A bus left a nearby stop, the diesel fumes making her cough through a haze.

"I read enough about the Blackstones to know you're in the family business." Chase's jaw flexed as he made the damning announcement. "That means you must be working a con."

Chase could see the dark cloud descend on Tana's pretty features, her brow furrowing as she scowled.

That was just as well.

He'd reached for the comment to resurrect a barrier after she'd kindled memories of their summer together. He'd enjoyed sharing his love of horseback riding with her, especially when she'd gravitated to it so naturally. But then, everything between them had felt easy, as if it had been destined.

Little did he know at the time that it only felt that way because con artists specialized in answering a need. They gained the trust of a mark, falling into the carefully set trap of the con.

And he'd fallen for it. For her.

Eight years hadn't erased the anger he had about that. So he'd be damned if he'd fall for Tana Blackstone's pretty smiles now. He knew better.

If there was still an attraction between them, then *he* would be the one to leverage it, not her. He wasn't getting played again.

Now, walking beside Fort Greene Park, they neared her building before she finally responded to his jab.

"My family doesn't dictate my work or my life choices." She clamped her hands into fists at her side, her stiff posture making her look as tough as her boots and studded belt suggested. "The only con I'm running now is the engagement *you* proposed."

They passed a group of about twenty step dancers working on their moves underneath the lights in a paved area of the park. The rhythmic stomp of their feet reminded him of line dancing.

Another pastime he'd introduced Tana to. Or thought he had.

Hell, she could have been born line dancing and horseback riding for all he knew.

Tension cranked through his forehead, and he resisted the urge to vise-grip his temples. "Maybe you should give me some pointers then, since you're the expert in deception." He slanted a glance her way, wondering how those painted-doll features of hers could hide such a shady side. "How are we going to pull this off?"

She exhaled a huff, and he swore he could almost see her breathing flames. "Fine. You want to know?"

She made a sharp turn down South Portland Avenue, stopping abruptly in front of the brownstone where she lived. When he'd hired a private investigator to track her down, Chase had researched Tana's life thoroughly enough to know the basics.

Her talents as an actress had won her the spot in the building. And he recalled that she currently shared the brownstone with two other women—a fashion stylist and a makeup artist.

He slowed to a stop after her, taking her measure. "I do."

Dropping her bag on the stoop, she leaned against the stone balustrade and glared at him.

"First, we need to consider our target." She brandished her index fingers, as if preparing to count off the steps. "Who's the mark in this case? Who are we trying to convince?"

"You're on a need-to-know basis for that." He had more than one mark in mind, but he couldn't help but hope that hearing of Tana's engagement to Chase would bring her father out of hiding.

She'd been right about that.

"Then we're already going into this without being prepared enough. It'll be on you if we can't pull this off." She stood with her hands on her hips. She was at least a half foot shorter than him but still ready to go toe-to-toe with him.

He fought the contrary urge to stroke her hair, wanting to sift the pink ends through his fingers.

"Maybe we should move on to the next tip for a successful con," he suggested in an easy tone, folding his arms as he leaned back against the opposite balustrade. "I understand that I'm responsible for messing up the first one."

"Fine. Second is that we both have to play our roles." She flashed two fingers, her middle one glinting with silver bands. "It doesn't matter how good an actress I am. If you're not playing your part, we'll never convince anyone we're a couple."

"You don't need to worry about me." He'd manage his business, the same way he always had. A relentless work ethic and good investment strategy had taken him from just barely getting by after Joe Blackstone sold off Cloverfield, to a second house in the Hamptons that supplemented his primary residence in Nevada. "I'll do my part."

She shook her head while a group of skateboarders wheeled past, their shouts and board tricks distracting them both for a moment before she spoke again.

"That's not even close to good enough. The best actress in the world can't do a believable scene for two by herself. You need to have your head in the role." She spouted the advice as if she were teaching a class on survival in the desert and the stakes were life and death.

But then, maybe that was how her father had taught her. He'd never thought much about what her life had been like before she'd helped deceive his family, but Chase felt a momentary curiosity before reminding himself he didn't want to empathize with this woman.

"I said, I'll do my part." Shoving away from the balustrade, he stepped closer to her. "I know how to make it believable."

Her brown eyes tracked his movements, her breath going shallow as he neared.

Yeah, he'd have to be dead not to notice the signs of her attraction. He still wrestled with his own.

"We don't even know each other anymore," she argued, her head tipping back a little to maintain eye contact.

His blood surged as he continued to close the distance, even while something in the depths of his brain warned him to step away.

"We probably never did." His gaze roamed her face from her widening eyes to the tight pucker of her frown. "But we should still know enough about each other to convince the world we're a couple."

His attention narrowed to her lips. He couldn't deny that he wanted a chance to relax that frown. Maybe make the rest of her loosen up, too.

"Impossible." She shook her head in denial, but her voice sounded breathless.

"Then let's start by convincing ourselves." He'd

dreamed of touching her so many times over the years. Kissing her. Tasting her.

Of course, the dreams started with torrid encounters and ended with him extracting revenge.

Taking back his lands and his pride.

"The last thing you want to do is believe your own con," she retorted softly, her melted-chocolate eyes dipping to his mouth.

"Then we'll have to walk that line carefully, won't we?" He cupped her chin in hand and pressed his thumb into her lower lip, rubbing the spot back and forth gently.

Like a lover.

Her eyelids fluttered.

He felt a sense of victory, causing a rush of adrenaline to surge through his system. That victory came at a cost, though, because she wasn't the only one affected by their nearness. It wasn't easy to stop himself from skimming his fingers into her hair and tugging her closer for a long, thorough taste.

But he couldn't allow Tana Blackstone to get the best of him this time, so he stepped back after a moment.

"Yes, we will," he answered his own question aloud, more than satisfied with what he'd learned here today. "I'll text you the travel plans tomorrow so you can make any needed arrangements for the weekend we're away."

She reached behind her to steady herself on the balustrade before taking a step away from him.

"I need to be back in town for a show rehearsal on

Monday." Tana peered at the doors to the brownstone before darting up the steps, grabbing her satchel on the way.

"You will be," he assured her, already looking forward to their next encounter.

And not just because she'd be signing over that property to him.

"Good." She gave a nod as she reached for the door, then stared back down at him. "And for what it's worth, *you* should be the one rehearsing before this weekend."

"Me? Is that right?"

"Definitely." She arched a brow at him, her tone derisive. "I didn't buy into that almost-kiss for a second."

He didn't have to hide a smile at her blatant lie, because before he knew it, she'd disappeared into the brownstone with a loud bang of the front door.

Three

Tana had barely crossed the threshold into the foyer when her friends rushed toward her from the adjoining great room.

"You've been holding out on us," her friend Sable Cordero accused in her southern Louisiana drawl, folding her arms in a way that drew attention to her baby bump. The hint of belly was a reminder that the fashion stylist would be moving out of the brownstone soon to begin her new life with her boss at the design house where she worked.

The stunning brunette had been engaged for four weeks, waiting to wed her baby daddy until the renovations on their nearby brownstone were completed. Even now, Sable spent her nights with him, but Tana had been happy her friend still passed as much time with her former roommates as she did.

"Seriously. Who is the hot cowboy?" Blair Westcott, a blue-eyed, platinum-blonde makeup artist who appeared to have descended from Vikings, took up the conversation as she planted her hands on her hips.

She wore faded jeans and a pink sweatshirt with the name of an upstate hospital facility emblazoned on the front, a place where she spent most of her weekends visiting her cancer warrior mom.

Tana had little in common with either of her roommates other than a fierce desire to make it in their respective competitive fields. They'd all gravitated to New York in the hope they could distinguish themselves in a place that could make or break talented people. Sable and Blair had come to her first show when she'd been cast in *A Streetcar Named Desire*, and they'd cheered the loudest. She loved that about her friends.

Even when they were being ridiculously nosy.

"It's not like that," she told them flatly, allowing her bag to fall to the limestone floor as a wave of exhaustion hit her.

Seeing Chase again may have had her senses buzzing, but now she felt faint as she thought about what she'd just agreed to. Had she really said she'd go to Nevada with him? As his fiancée?

"Oh?" Sable circled her, narrowing her hazel eyes as she studied Tana. "Flushed cheeks. Aura of frazzled agitation. Breathing too fast. I'd say you're showing all the symptoms of something intriguing happening between you and the cowboy."

"Sable and I were just sitting by the front window, drinking a pregnant-mother-approved tea blend and minding our own business, when a man strolled up Portland Avenue like a gunslinger out of an old Western." Blair fanned herself with one hand. "Did you see the shoulders on that man?"

Tana felt her cheeks heat more, even though she had no reason to feel anything about any of this, damn it.

"Aren't you two supposed to be in committed relationships?" She raised both arms in exasperation and marched past them to drop into one of the easy chairs near the front windows. She made a point of lowering the blinds so the view to the street was shut out. "What do you care what he looks like?"

Her friends followed her into the great room, the scent of popcorn drifting up from the kitchen telling her that there'd been a recent batch made. Her stomach growled, reminding her that she would have normally gone out to dinner by now with her castmates.

"I fell in love, Tana," Blair explained patiently, referring to the new man in her life. She dropped down onto one rolled arm of Tana's chair. "I didn't lose my senses. So how do you know him? Details, please."

Sable sat on the other chair arm so that Tana was bracketed by her friends. Their presence comforted her even as they tried to drag answers out of her. The realization of how much she'd grown to rely on these women in the short time they'd known one another had her chest tightening unexpectedly.

Growing up, friends were a luxury she couldn't afford because of her family's lifestyle. They'd never remained in one place for too long, so there'd been no opportunities to forge deeper connections. And even if there had been time, she couldn't confide anything about herself, not when she'd been part of a criminal enterprise. From a very young age, she'd known that her family wasn't like other people's.

So having Sable and Blair poking her for answers because they loved her? Maybe it wasn't so bad. She just didn't know how to tell them the story without revealing a criminal past…something she really wasn't ready to share.

"Okay." She huffed out a long breath and sat straighter in the chair, scooting up to sit on the edge. "Here's the deal. Chase Serrano was my first everything. First love. First boyfriend. First heartbreak… you get the idea. Basically, I screwed up with him, he hated me for it, I moved away, and we never spoke again until today."

There was a beat of silence, making her look up at her friends' faces to see their reactions.

Blair frowned, her blond eyebrows knit together. Sable reared back like she couldn't understand what Tana had said.

"You are a colossal failure at storytelling," Sable announced. "Shouldn't the ability to hold an audience be part of an actor's gift?"

Blair turned on the arm of the chair so that she

faced Tana fully. "You don't want to tell us what happened in the past. That's okay." She lounged sideways, leaning an elbow into the chair back as if there would be lots more talking to come. "Just tell us what happened today."

Sable mirrored the posture, propping herself on her elbow and resting her dark head on her palm. "Right. How did he find you after hating you for so long? Or maybe more importantly, *why* did he want to find you?"

"And did he ride a horse into Brooklyn Bridge Park at any time?" Blair wanted to know.

Tana slumped back in the easy chair again, so that their heads were all just inches apart for this conversation. She was the one clearly in the hot seat, but she still found herself wishing she had her video camera rolling to record the moment. She could imagine exactly how she'd block the scene to have all three faces in the shot. She'd have proof on film that she had friends. Good friends who believed in her.

Closing her eyes, she allowed herself to mentally record what was happening. Somehow, the trick made it easier to talk.

"Picture this. Me on stage, delivering my final killer line as Blanche DuBois. I walk off, all smiles and sunshine. Then I return for the bows and I see him, front and center in the lower orchestra seats." She didn't bother to explain where that was in a theater. Her friends had helped her rehearse enough times that they knew more than they ever wanted to about the theater world. "The sexiest man I've ever

met, Stetson and all, glaring at me like he's come to dole out vengeance for my…past transgressions."

She couldn't bring herself to share her past with them. Couldn't jeopardize the good opinions they had of her.

"Oh. Shivers," Blair said softly.

"I take back what I said about your storytelling," Sable added from Tana's other side. "What did you do?"

"Duh. I ran off stage as fast as possible and thought I made a clean getaway." Tana wondered if he'd seen her the whole time. He'd probably clocked the Airstream trailer before he even watched the show. "Then suddenly there he was, walking me home because he came to New York specifically for me. To…settle an old score."

She forced her eyes open, knowing she couldn't just dream away the reality of what had transpired between them. Her gaze flipped from Blair's face to Sable's. Both women were watching her intently.

Both cared.

Her belly tightened at the thought of them finding out about her past. All the ways she'd hurt and disappointed people by being a Blackstone.

"What does that mean for you?" Sable asked. "Can you help this guy—Chase—with whatever it is that he wants?"

"Sure I can." She shoved to her feet, knowing that she couldn't afford to confide much more than that today. With any luck, she'd go to Nevada, sign over the land, and that would be the end of it. No harm, no foul. Her friends never had to know what she'd done to deserve Chase's anger. "I just have to fly to Nevada with him this weekend and pretend I'm his fiancée."

Jaws dropped.

When her friends recovered, the questions commenced.

"Is it to get a matchmaking mother off his back?" Sable proposed. "In the books I read, that's usually the reason someone wants to have a fake engagement."

Blair didn't give Tana time to answer before she pitched another possibility. "Or maybe he needs a fiancée to secure an inheritance from a rich relative. That's pretty old-school, but people can attach all kinds of crazy caveats to their wills."

"Honestly, I'm not sure." Tana knew he had an ulterior motive. He'd admitted to more than one. But she was at a disadvantage with him because she hadn't kept tabs on him over the years and didn't know much about how his life had changed. She needed to address that lack of knowledge before she saw him again and get busy with some research. "But I owe him a favor after the way things ended between us. So if he needs me to be a pretend fiancée, so be it. I'll be back in time for show rehearsal on Monday, and that's all that matters."

Her friends lobbied energetically for more details, but in the end, she convinced them to make dinner with her and drop the discussion for now. Grateful for the reprieve, she soaked up the time with them,

knowing the whole while that her days of living outside the shadow of her past were numbered.

Midway through the flight from New York to the airport in Elko, Nevada, Chase studied his lone traveling companion from across the aisle of a friend's private plane.

He'd sent Tana the flight details two days ago, and she'd texted him back a single word of acknowledgment, making him wary that she'd back out of their agreement. But sure enough, she'd shown up on time in the car he'd sent for her to begin their cross-country venture. After choosing a spot on the eight-seat Gulfstream, she'd withdrawn a tablet from her lone bag and directed her attention to the screen.

Chase had let her be, reading her back-off vibe loud and clear, even without the ominous new tattoos designed to look like superhero bangles on her wrists. He'd been surprised to see the fresh ink at first, until he realized on closer inspection—okay, maybe he hadn't ignored her after all—that her tattoos were henna. Those that he'd noticed three days ago had faded a little. The bangles she'd added were darker. All of them looked hand-drawn, making him curious if she did them herself.

Making him even more curious to know if she had additional designs elsewhere on her body.

Dragging his thoughts from such tempting speculation, he continued to take her in. She'd refreshed the pink strands in her glossy brown hair since he'd seen her last. She'd ditched the clunky combat boots in favor of pink high-top sneakers completely covered with silver spikes. Combined with her black skinny jeans and a worn T-shirt from a West Coast Day of the Dead festival, she'd clearly dressed to send a message.

But he refused to allow himself to be distracted by something so superficial. The first time he'd met Tana, she'd turned his head so thoroughly he had missed what was happening right under his nose in his mother's life. If he'd learned one thing eight years ago, it was not to fall for misdirection. When a con artist drew your attention to what was in the right hand, you'd damned well better look at what was in the left.

With that in mind, he steeled himself for conversation. Now that they neared their weekend destination, he needed to outline a few ground rules to keep things on track. He was in charge of how things shook down at Cloverfield this time.

Chase reached into his jacket to produce the ring box he'd stashed when a photo on Tana's tablet screen caught his eye.

A picture of him.

"You're googling me?" he found himself asking in spite of his efforts not to let her distract him.

Tana didn't even glance his way. She kept her head down, attention ostensibly focused on the screen, though her hair hid her features from view.

"Just trying to even the odds," she murmured offhandedly, trailing a finger over the tablet to scroll down a page. She wore a delicate chain around her

wrist that connected to a second chain around her middle finger. The jewelry had one silver charm of an eye that lay flat on the back of her hand. "You know everything about me since we parted, but I know nothing about you. This consumer education website you put together, for example, is all news to me."

Chase forced his gaze away from her to stare out the plane window. Thin wisps of clouds seem to cling to the aircraft.

"Since I gained no satisfaction from mounting a civil suit against your missing father, I thought I'd at least warn other vulnerable people about the kinds of scam artists out there." His research on the subject had been appalling. "It's disheartening to learn how many ways people avoid honest labor by cheating their neighbors."

A beat of silence followed his words. But when Tana spoke again, she didn't bother arguing with him.

"And it looks like your ex-girlfriend is getting married this weekend." Tana recrossed her legs in a way that put one pink-sneakered foot in the aisle between them. "How is Ashley, anyway?"

Irritation flared in Chase, both at the mention of the other woman's name and at the reminder that Tana had once known so much about him. He'd confided in her about his complicated relationship with the daughter of the richest man in the northern half of the state. Ashley Carmichael was a spoiled daddy's girl, used to having her own way. She'd taken it poorly when Chase had broken things off to be with Tana. So, too, had her powerful father. Warren Carmichael had swindled him at cards when Chase was at his lowest point in life. And the bastard had continued doing everything he could to sabotage Chase's business interests ever since.

So Chase had been more than a little surprised to receive an invitation to his former girlfriend's nuptials.

"You'll find out soon enough." He reached into his pocket again, ready to put the next step of his plan in motion. "But you'll need this first."

He thrust the ring box across the aisle to her, setting it on top of her tablet without touching her. After the almost-kiss in front of her brownstone earlier in the week, he knew his resistance to this woman's touch was not as strong as he would have preferred.

She swung surprised eyes toward him. "I hope you're not suggesting there's a visit with your horrible ex-girlfriend in my future."

He arched an eyebrow. Letting her put the pieces together for herself.

Her jaw dropped open a moment later.

"Oh. My. God." Tana gripped the ring box in one fist without opening it. Without taking her fathomless brown gaze off him. "*Please* do not tell me that you dragged me all the way across the country to attend Ashley Freaking Carmichael's wedding with you."

"You're perfectly dressed for it, actually." In a week full of vengeance schemes and righting the wrongs of his past, Chase could hardly be blamed for taking whatever pleasure he could out of the situation. And the vision of Tana in her new tough-girl incarnation on his arm this weekend was definitely cause for a grin. "I'd take great personal satisfaction if you show up to the reception in studded pink high tops."

She scowled hard at him, banging the ring box against her tablet like a gavel. "You asked me to straighten out the land deal, not mince around some society princess's bridezilla nightmare."

"You don't need to mince," he assured her, unexpectedly glad to have someone on his arm tomorrow who would dread the company as much as him. "And you knew that I had more than one reason for asking you to pose as my fiancée. This is one of them."

She huffed out a long breath, her glare fading by degrees, replaced by a fleeting look of genuine worry.

That expression, however brief, stirred apprehension. He might want to settle a debt with Tana for her deceit, but at the moment, it occurred to him he didn't want to cause the kind of pain he'd just glimpsed.

A moment later, her face cleared. "Fine. But I'm not going to play Cinderella for you to dress me up in fancy clothes when I don't want to attend this thing in the first place."

"And you call yourself an actress?" he teased. "But no worries. I don't think I'd know how to carry over your aesthetic into formalwear anyhow."

Once again, she didn't take the bait, making him aware that by being petty, he revealed too much of his own bitterness. Even now, after he'd schooled himself on the tactics of con artists, he'd forgotten one of the most important rules: keep personal feelings out of it.

The woman next to him sure did.

"I can play a role for you, Chase." The seriousness in her tone had him reevaluating her. No matter what message her new look sent to the world, there was an extremely clever, clearheaded woman beneath the facade. "But I need to understand the objective first."

"No." He refused to bring her into his plans. "I can't trust you with that. It's enough that you're by my side tomorrow. I want Warren Carmichael to think we're a couple, and that we've been back together for months."

She nodded. "I can do that. But I need some particulars so we keep our stories straight. How did we meet up again?"

Her keen attention reminded him of old times. When he'd taught her how to ride, she hadn't just jumped on the back of a horse. She'd taken time to learn how to care for an animal. How to saddle it properly and speak soothingly to it.

Out of the blue, he suddenly recalled that he'd remarked on her attention to those details. She'd told him that she'd had so few possessions in life that it had taught her to be respectful with the things she had, and anything she cared for even temporarily. For a long time, he'd dismissed everything she'd said to him during that summer as lies. But now he wondered if that had been true.

Or was her concern about his goal this weekend just another smokescreen?

"Let's keep it simple. How about we say that I met you at a play you were doing?" He wasn't worried about a cover story since he didn't plan to stick around the wedding for long. He just wanted to make an appearance to put Warren Carmichael on notice.

The plane bumped along an air pocket, causing Chase to reach across the aisle on instinct. His hand landed on her forearm before he recalled what a bad idea it was to touch her.

Already, his fingers flexed automatically, seeking more of her smooth skin before he hauled his hand away again.

She glanced down at her arm where his fingers had been just a moment before. Then she shook her head.

"*Streetcar* is my first real show, though, and it only started four weeks ago. How about we say I looked you up at your office downtown after I read about you online? I sought you out to apologize for the past and we—you know." Her eyes found his, heat flickering in their depths. "Reconnected."

The temperature spiked between them as memories flooded his brain. They'd shared hot, passionate nights that lasted into the next day. Their affair had been all-consuming. It took him several moments to get his tongue unstuck enough to answer her.

"Yeah. We'll go with that." His voice rasped with

the remembered attraction. He needed to move the conversation away from those dangerous thoughts. "You should put the ring on. We'll be landing soon."

He didn't even watch as she cracked open the lid on the box, the hinges making a soft sound. Chase closed his eyes for the landing, reminding himself this weekend was not about the connection he still felt with Tana Blackstone.

It wasn't about remembering how soft her lips were when she kissed him. Or how fully she surrendered herself to him in his arms. Or how he'd never found any other woman to match her. None of his relationships since her had compared, and how messed up was that when his relationship with Tana hadn't even been real?

He was simply bringing her to Nevada to help him recover the rest of what she'd stolen from him. Once that was done, he'd make the most of the engagement to lure her father back to American soil to finally face legal and civil charges.

Then he could walk away for good.

Four

An hour later, seated in Chase's Ford pickup truck that was so big she'd practically needed a stepladder to haul herself into it, Tana stared down at the breathtaking engagement ring on her finger. The late-day sun shot prisms of light off the facets as they approached Cloverfield Ranch.

Chase had passed the ring to her with such a total lack of ceremony—slapping the box onto her tablet back on the plane—that she hadn't been sure how to react. Especially when she'd seen the cushion-cut double halo ring with pink diamonds in platinum. It was a description she would have never called up from her personal knowledge, but a quick photo sent in a group text to Sable and Blair had revealed the details, set off with dozens of exclamation points and heart emojis.

Tana only knew it was gorgeous. And for the life of her, she couldn't understand why Chase would put her in possession of something so valuable when he clearly thought she was little better than a common thief. Maybe he was trying to trap her into bolting with the thing, then have her arrested.

With a sigh, she returned to the view of the dramatic Humboldt Range outside the pickup's windshield as they neared their destination.

Her fingers twitched over her bag with the need to find her camcorder and capture what she saw, but how would that look to her surly and silent travel companion? No doubt he'd accuse her of wanting to commemorate a con or something equally dire, which hurt more than it should. In truth, she simply wished to hold this image in her mind, the soaring mountains serving as a backdrop to green hillsides dotted with grazing brown cows. The colors were so rich it looked like someone had turned on a filter to enhance them. Something about the expansive vistas made her want to take deep, healing breaths, as if the air alone could soothe a soul.

Foolishness, really, considering this was the site of one of her father's worst crimes. She should feel uneasy, perhaps, sensing that Chase grew more agitated the closer they came to Cloverfield. Yet all she felt at the moment was a satisfied sense that she hadn't dreamed how stunning this place had been. In the intervening years, she'd sometimes wondered if she'd only imagined the magnetic draw of it, her vision too influenced by how happy she'd been during the brief months she'd spent here.

But she hadn't dreamed it. The remote corner of northern Nevada where Cloverfield sat remained the most spectacularly beautiful place she'd ever seen.

"Anything look familiar yet?" Chase's voice called her from her musing as he downshifted before the turnoff to a private road.

If Tana's friends had thought he looked like a Western gunslinger when they saw him three days ago, she wondered what they'd say if they spotted him now. Dressed in dark jeans that clung to strong thighs, Chase wore boots and a fitted Western shirt in a shade of gray that made his eyes look almost silver. He hadn't worn his black Stetson on the plane, but it went on his head the moment they'd stepped on the tarmac, and it remained there now, shading those stormy eyes. The Patek Philippe watch he'd worn in the city had been replaced with a sturdy-looking vintage piece with a thick leather strap.

"Of course I recognize the area." Attempting to keep her tone neutral, she wasn't ready to let him see all the ways this drive had already affected her when she hadn't worked out her emotions for herself yet. No matter what her father had done here, this was the place where Tana had known more happiness than any other. "The cabin Dad rented that summer is up here on the left."

Her stomach tightened, preparing for a barb about her father. She understood Chase's anger. He was entitled to it. She just wished he didn't color her with the same brush as her felon parent. Chase would never understand how hard she'd worked to separate herself from the past.

"Not anymore, it isn't." He slowed the truck for the rougher road they now traveled. "The first thing I did when I bought back the land was raze the building."

She blinked at the harshness of the sentence for a house that was—after all—an inanimate object and not responsible for her father's crime. A moment later, the spot where the cabin should have stood came into view. The old horseshoe driveway remained, along with the western juniper tree that used to shade the front bedroom that had once been hers.

But the small log structure was gone. In its place, a handful of work vehicles were parked in the shade of the juniper. A dump truck and utility van were flanked by pickups with beds full of orange cones, shovels and a couple of wheelbarrows.

"I'm surprised you could tear it down. I was under the impression it was historic." She knew much of the ranch dated from the 1800s, including the stone-block home where Chase's mother had lived.

"It's not as old as it looks. I just had to pull a permit to take it down, and the appraiser's office confirmed the structure was more recent." Chase shifted again, one knuckle grazing her knee. "Less than a century old."

The warmth of his hand against the denim sent a bolt of reaction through her thigh, tickling her in places that had gone a long, long time without tickling of any kind.

This was going to be a rough weekend if she couldn't rein that in.

She crossed her legs. Tightly.

"So you didn't destroy any history, you just tore down something perfectly good to make way for something fancier. Sounds like the Hamptons are wearing off on you."

His chuckle surprised her. "As it happened, I made a nice chunk of change selling the reclaimed wood from the cabin. There's a good market for wood that looks like it has a history even if it doesn't."

"Sort of like me." She propped an elbow on the truck door and kept her gaze trained outside. Away from her ex-lover and the appealing sound of his laughter. "I may appear to have a suspect past when I'm actually just the offspring of criminals. Looks can be deceiving, you know."

When he didn't answer at first, she assumed he wasn't going to reply. But after passing an equipment barn and what used to be the foreman's house, Chase finally cleared his throat.

"I am aware of that." He glanced over at her, the weight of his stare making the fine hairs on the back of her neck stand up even though she kept her attention fixed outside. "Logically, I understand you can't be held responsible for your father's actions."

"And yet you blame me." She hadn't expected him to have some big epiphany about her this weekend, but she couldn't help feeling frustrated that he wanted to remind her at every turn that he held the past against her. "Considering we have to get through a wedding tomorrow as a couple, it might help build the illusion of romance if you quit reminding me I'm the root of all your misfortune."

"Right. Agreed." The sincerity in his voice had her turning her head to look at him.

Sure enough, he appeared almost…chastened?

"Really?" She shifted on the seat as the main house came into sight. "You think I'm right?"

Parking the vehicle, Chase switched off the ignition and gave her his undivided attention.

"I took your advice to heart when we spoke that evening outside your brownstone. You said I needed to prepare for my role, and I plan to do just that."

"Well then. That's good." She smoothed a nervous hand through her hair, unsure how to respond. She'd been so busy bracing for confrontational Chase that she suddenly had no clue how to cope with cooperative Chase.

"You said we should practice being a couple," he reminded her, moving one long arm to rest along the back of her seat.

Not touching her. But the nearness of his hand, the *potential* for touching, sent a little shock wave through her system.

"I—don't think that's what I said." Memories of the almost-kiss loomed large in her brain.

That moment had started out like this one. They'd been face-to-face then, too. Her knees had gone weak that day when he cupped her chin, tilting her face up to his. Embarrassingly, she'd about chewed her bottom lip raw that night in an unconscious effort to taste him where he'd touched her.

"Maybe you said we should *rehearse* our role as a couple," he clarified, pushing up the brim of his Stetson a fraction with the passing of his thumb over his forehead. "Either way, the implication was clear."

Her heart thumped so loudly she suspected she'd missed approximately every other word out of his mouth. In New York, she deflected men as easily as breathing, with a prickly vibe built into everything about her appearance and manner. But the skill eluded her with Chase, as if her body refused to transmit the don't-touch signals she sent to everyone else.

It was annoying.

"What implication?" She stared, wide-eyed, at him.

"That we should get comfortable around each other." He reached across the truck cab to lay his palm on her knee. The warm weight anchored her to the spot even as it kicked her pulse into a staccato beat.

She might have protested the casual way he touched her—deftly setting fire to her senses even as he seemed unaffected—except her tongue remained glued to the roof of her mouth.

"You had a good point about that," he continued, his thumb sliding back and forth along the seam of denim just inside her knee.

A caress that should not have been so damned potent.

Focus.

"Are you regarding this as rehearsal?" she finally managed, glancing down at his wandering hand. "Because I'm not sure winding me up is the same thing as making me feel comfortable around you."

His thumb went still as his gray eyes darkened.

"I look forward to hearing all about the difference after we get settled." His voice smoked along her senses before he eased back.

Then, after opening the driver's-side door, he exited the vehicle, leaving her hot and bothered as well as confused. She hated not knowing his endgame for this engagement, but she couldn't deny that being around him again aroused her.

That was dangerous for her peace of mind.

So when he opened the passenger door to help her down, Tana was careful to let go of his hand the moment her feet hit the ground. She might be a good actress, but if Chase kept touching her this weekend, she couldn't possibly pretend to be unaffected.

Everything about having Tana back at Cloverfield Ranch felt surreal.

Chase wandered the exposed stone hallways of his historic birthplace while he waited for her to unpack and settle into the guest room. He'd only brought her into his childhood home a couple of times when they'd been dating that long-ago summer. He'd lived in the bunkhouse he was remodeling, for one thing.

Only his mother had resided in the main house. Besides, Chase and Tana had spent more time horseback riding or hiking. Occasionally, they'd attended bonfires and picnics with other locals close to their own age.

But he'd made dinner for both Tana and his mother once in this house. Tana had stayed afterward to help him clean up, and then they'd slow-danced around the firepit in the backyard. Another time, Tana had brought his mother wildflowers she'd picked on one of their hikes, and Chase had been convinced his then-girlfriend would be in his life for years to come.

A doorknob turned in the room down the hallway, wrenching him from memories he didn't want to revisit now.

Tana peeked out the doorway, a scowl furrowing her forehead. "Hey, Serrano. I thought I said I wasn't going to play Cinderella this weekend."

He'd known she would give him flak about the evening wear he'd stocked in the wardrobe for her since he hadn't warned her about the wedding. He pretended interest in the view out the gabled window at the far end of the corridor, keeping his tone easy.

"Suit yourself if you want to wear the high tops," he told her blandly. "Or else I can drive you into downtown Elko tomorrow to see what you can purchase off the rack. Though, keep in mind, they may not have the selection you're used to in New York."

He turned toward her while she made a garbled

sound of exasperation, vanishing into the room as she continued to speak.

"You realize every outfit in here looks straight out of the cartoon princess collection?" She reappeared on the threshold of the door, thrusting out a gold gown on a padded hanger. "Look at this."

The garment was beautiful by any standards. A handmade designer original. He wouldn't know how to describe it, but the layers of beaded tulle and the floral embroidery spoke of careful craftsmanship.

"Is it the wrong size?" He slowly walked toward her, trying to get his bearings in the conversation. All the while, he kept thinking about how lovely she looked with her hair piled on top of her head, a pair of cat-eye glasses on her nose, the frames a pink leopard print. "I fail to see what's wrong with it."

"What's wrong?" She clutched the waist to her slender middle and stared down at the effect of the gown pressed to her body. "I'll look entirely too precious for anyone to believe I'm not playing a part."

He stopped just shy of the door frame, the white-washed guest room already bearing a hint of her citrus and amber fragrance even though she'd cracked the windows overlooking the backyard, letting the scent of fresh-cut hay into the room. Behind her, he saw the contents of her dark leather overnight bag spilled on the white duvet, a few T-shirts tangled with jeans and a black lace lingerie set that had him mentally undressing her so he could imagine it on her.

"I see what you mean," he forced himself to say

past a dry throat. "Maybe you can accessorize with a spiked collar and boots."

Her gaze flew to his, her dark eyes assessing him through the funky glasses. She frowned for a moment, then huffed out a long sigh.

"Sorry for being an ingrate. The gowns are beautiful and I'm sure I'll find something suitable for the wedding." She backed deeper into the room before opening the door of the rustic cypress wardrobe and hanging the dress inside.

She withdrew a pink dress and held it up for inspection.

"Wait a minute. What just happened there?" He dragged his gaze from the lingerie—how had it returned to the black lace without his permission?—and watched Tana. "You went from railing at me over the gowns to thanking me."

"I'm practicing what I preach." She padded over to the bed and laid down the gown to study it, her bare feet with pink toenails a curiously intimate sight. "I'm letting you see more sides of my personality so you're comfortable with me tomorrow when we have to be a couple in public. I do have an agreeable side, you know."

He wasn't sure how much to believe her anymore between her acting skills, her past as a grifter and her vaguely hostile attitude toward him. An attitude he was no doubt responsible for inciting.

But now that he was close to achieving the first of his objectives in the form of attending the wedding with Tana, Chase was prepared to cultivate a facade of romance and passion with her.

Not that they'd be sticking around the reception long enough to show it off. But why not reap some pleasure during this time together since the attraction between them was—to his surprise and confusion—still very much alive.

"I appreciate that." He stepped over the threshold into the guest room while she straightened the tangle of other clothes still cluttering the bed. "Both the agreeable aspect and the effort required to bring it to the fore."

His heart slugged heavily against the inside of his chest at his proximity to her. He stopped near the foot of the old-fashioned wrought-iron bedstead, his gaze dropping to the curve of her neck bared by the way she'd pinned her hair in a twist.

She'd changed into an oversize lounge T-shirt while she unpacked, the ivory boatneck collar slipping off one shoulder. There was something vulnerable-looking about the back of a neck. Something that made him want to step behind her and shield her. Right before he kissed the spot.

He breathed in the fresh air drifting through the cracked window in an attempt to cool himself down.

"If you don't love the clothes, you should take it up with your roommate," he found himself saying, fingers reaching through the wrought iron to smooth a silk ruffle hem on the pink gown that lay discarded there, one of six he'd requested so that she had a choice of wardrobe for the wedding.

"Excuse me?" She swung to face him, planting her fists on her hips.

"I read the articles about how you won the spot in your apartment, and there were profiles of your roommates online. One makeup artist. One fashion stylist." No doubt he'd read more about Tana Blackstone than was strictly necessary.

He shouldn't have found her movements after she left Nevada so interesting, but his curiosity had been avid. And now that he stood before the woman herself—as intrigued by her as ever—he had to ask himself if he'd craved this meeting with her as much as he craved vengeance.

"Blair and Sable," she murmured, half to herself. Then, lifting an eyebrow, she cocked her head to one side. "You spoke to them?"

"I messaged with the stylist and asked if I could hire her services to assist with a wardrobe for you this weekend. She seemed very enthusiastic."

Her eyes narrowed. "Are you telling me she knew I was attending a wedding before I did?"

"She did. She commented that she's been dreaming of dressing you. Her exact words." He'd trusted her friend to at least know Tana's sizes, but Sable Cordero had proven keenly efficient at her job, sending shoes and accessories along with the outfits from a handful of fashion houses, including the designer she worked for.

"That explains a lot," she muttered drily as she refolded a T-shirt, the engagement ring he'd given her casting sparkles in the sunlight. "I'll remember who to blame when I show up at the reception looking like Elsa. Now, if only I knew who I'm putting on the fiancée show for."

He ground his teeth at the thought of seeing his local nemesis. But the time had come to share the target with her.

"Ashley's father. Warren Carmichael." Briefly, he outlined how the man had tied up thousands of Chase's acres in a baseless land dispute, contesting grazing permits and bringing the federal Bureau of Land Management down on Chase's head. "I've spent a small fortune on legal fees already, but Warren seems determined to undermine me as often as possible."

While he spoke, Tana had given up all pretense of organizing her clothes. She looked up at him now with thoughtful brown eyes. "So how will it help to have me as your fiancée?"

"Remember the piece of land that you're signing over to me?" He wondered if Joe Blackstone had any idea how valuable that particular piece of property was. If he had, wouldn't he have clued in his daughter somehow in the intervening years?

Suspicion simmered in the back of his mind even while he battled a fierce attraction to the woman beside him. He remembered how her eyelashes had fluttered when he'd touched her knee in the truck earlier, and knew that the chemistry between them was a caress away from igniting again.

"Of course I do." She nodded, full lips pursed.

"About half of it is at the center of the dispute be-

tween Warren and me. He's had an investigator trying to discover the identity of the owner for as long
as I have. I just found you sooner."

She shook her head, the hair twisted at the back
of her head wobbling with the motion. "I still don't
see how it makes any earthly difference if we're engaged since I volunteered to sign it all over to you
in the first place."

Maybe it was because they'd been standing next
to a bed this whole time, but her declaration sent a
surge of longing through him. Something about her
willingness to do what he wanted sparked the latent
attraction until it blazed up his spine.

"Warren will stop at nothing to win the personal
war against me." He resented everything about
Chase, from the time he'd broken things off with
Warren's daughter, to the audacity of Chase's bid
to regain lands Warren had run roughshod over for
a decade, grazing his cattle illegally. "That could
mean he would harass you in ways I can't predict.
Our engagement sends a message up front that you're
under my protection. Also that I've already won this
round."

He'd edged closer to her while he spoke, more
than ready to test the authenticity of their connection before they put it on public display.

"Ah. How very caveman of you. I'm a symbolic
prize, then." She licked her upper lip as he neared
her, a quick, nervous swipe.

Or was that anticipation?

"To the victor belong the spoils." He wasn't sure

why he said it when he hadn't planned to rile her up. He just wanted to kiss that spot she'd licked.

But getting under her skin let him see more of her character. She revealed more about herself when he baited her.

"I'll certainly be dressed like a hapless war prize if I wear one of the dresses Sable chose." She fingered a loose lock of hair that trailed along her neck, not sounding terribly upset about the role he wanted her to play. "But I draw the line at being carried off and ravished."

"I never suggested any such thing," he reminded her, reaching to take the lock of hair from her fingers so he could repeat the action. He smoothed the strands between his thumb and forefinger, rubbing the silky length. "Although I find it gratifying your mind went there. I was thinking more along the lines of a kiss than a full-on ravishing. But I could be persuaded."

The fire in her eyes leaped as she tipped her head up to look at him. A vein in her neck throbbed with a fast-pounding pulse and he wanted nothing so much as to cover that spot with his lips. To feel the warmth of her on his tongue.

"Is this another game for you? Trying to make me feel some of the old draw between us?"

They were so close now he could feel her soft exhales on his knuckles where he toyed with her glossy dark hair.

"This is no game. I want to kiss you, Tana. So very much."

She gripped the shoulders of his shirt, tugging him closer still. "Then for crying out loud, please hurry up."

Five

Tana didn't wait for an answer.

One second she was talking to Chase beside the bed in the guest room. The next she propelled herself up against him, flying into his arms to press her mouth to his.

Heat rushed through her limbs, circled her chest, pooled deep in her belly as their lips met. The past merged with the present; her best memories all included this man and the kind of kisses he'd taught her during one unforgettable summer.

She'd never gotten him out of her head. They'd been so young, but he'd been the first to kiss her like she was a woman. The first to show her the wonder of her own body. She'd gone on to compare every man to him afterward, and no one had come close to matching the heat and passion he inspired.

He did not disappoint now, either.

While she arched into him with an urgency that surely communicated how much she wanted him, Chase seemed to channel all his energies on delivering the perfect mating of mouths. His tongue stroked over her lips in a way that had her trembling, partly because the memories of that first kiss were still so potent.

But also because Chase at twenty-six years old was a different sensory experience than Chase at eighteen. The lithe grace of youth had hardened into steely muscle that flexed and shifted against her as he moved. The gentle scrape of his jaw—cleanly shaven when she'd first met him this morning—was shadowed with bristles when she ran a hand along his face.

His lips were as gentle as ever, though. His tongue every bit as sensual, teasing hers into a dance that slowly set her on fire through a delicious give-and-take. Stroking. Licking. Sucking lightly.

She gripped his shoulders through the cotton button-down, needing an anchor when she feared she might float away on a tide of longing.

Longing for heat. Connection. A moment when she felt like she could be herself and not have to put up a facade…

At that thought, her blood chilled. She forced herself back a step, breaking the kiss. Shattering the moment.

"What are we doing?"

The words were wheezed out from burning lungs. Possibly she'd forgotten to breathe while Chase kissed her.

Coming back to herself, she took in his gray eyes, still a little molten. Other than that, she saw no sign of the inferno that had just scorched her inside and out.

"I think we were preparing ourselves for tomorrow." He backed up a step, scratching his thumb along his forehead while he seemed to contemplate her.

Her heart still galloped too fast. Her lips tingled where his mouth had met hers. The urge to touch the spot was almost overwhelming, but she managed to turn her attention back to the task of organizing her things.

She needed to keep her hands busy to prevent herself from touching Chase again.

"Did we learn anything useful?" she asked, shaking out a folded shirt so she could fold it again.

"Only that we won't have to fake the sparks between us." He backed up another step, nearing the door. "That part comes naturally enough."

She swung her head toward him to gauge his expression. He appeared sincere if a bit rueful.

Yeah. She related.

Without answering, she returned to her task, giving her full attention to relocating her underwear to a dresser drawer.

He paused at the threshold of her door. "I'll leave

you to get settled. The groom in the stable will help you if you'd like to ride later. Dinner is at seven."

"Thank you. A ride sounds nice actually." She hadn't been on horseback since she left Cloverfield, and she'd missed it.

Or maybe she just missed anything that she used to do with Chase Serrano and the fleeting, fragile happiness she'd once felt with him.

Should she invite him to ride with her? She opened her mouth to frame the question, but her companion had already gone.

The hallway outside her room remained silent, but Tana's nerves were jangled as she recalled the way that kiss had made her feel. Chase was the only man who'd ever quieted her insides to the point where she didn't feel like an imposter in life.

Sadly, he only wanted her for her ability to play a role. And she would be wise to remember that.

Dressed in his wedding guest finery the next afternoon, Chase extended his hand to help Tana from the hired Land Rover in front of Briar Creek Ranch, home of his local nemesis.

"This is a private residence?" Her brown eyes were wide as she took in everything from the valet service implemented for the special occasion to the scale of the main ranch house near the pristine barn built solely as a special events venue.

"Believe it or not, yes. This is a working cattle ranch, but Warren Carmichael purposely overbuilt the place so he could always host his political cronies." Chase's gaze swept over Tana in her cream silk gown printed with big roses, a small train attached to the fitted sheath.

Her pink pumps and square clutch were equally elegant, but he'd noticed she wore a thin band of cream-colored leather strapped around one wrist that featured tiny gold spikes. The piece was so narrow it blended with a collection of more traditional chains encircling the same wrist. How well her friend must know Tana to have sent the accessory that was a throwback to the style she normally embraced.

She looked so stunning, in fact, he sort of wished she'd gone with the jeans and high tops. Although considering how many times he'd relived the kiss they shared the night before, he suspected he would have found her appealing no matter what.

"Clearly he's done well for himself," Tana observed. "I've seen luxury venues in Las Vegas that weren't this elaborate." She allowed him to tuck her hand into his elbow for the walk down the red carpet that led from the valet stand toward the nearby barn, where the huge doors were thrown open to guests.

Mellow country music sounded inside the barn, the strains of a fiddle blending with the crooning of a female singer as guests began arriving for the reception. On the hill outside the barn, Chase could see liveried waitstaff passing hors d'oeuvres and trays of champagne to guests milling around. He smoothed a hand down the lapel of his classic black Tom Ford tuxedo as he leaned closer to Tana to speak more quietly.

"Warren has sealed more than one deal favorable to his land by inviting key local figures to the ranch for weekends spent shooting and playing cards." Chase warded off the old fury about one card game in particular while he tracked the guests mingling under a juniper tree off to one side of the barn. He needed to mentally prepare himself for whatever Carmichael had up his sleeve today.

Their enmity had never been a secret over the last eight and a half years, so Chase couldn't be sure why Warren had invited him in the first place. Unless Ashley just wanted to flaunt her marriage to some rich dude. Not that Chase cared.

Beside him, Tana stiffened. "Cards? I hope you know I don't play." She made a small sound of disgust. "Not anymore, at least."

Chase didn't plan to address that statement at the moment, clearly a jab to get a reaction from him, maybe even start an argument that would let her off the hook as his date. She was by his side today, and that was enough. He wouldn't push her about the role he hoped she'd play in the rest of his agenda.

Especially not when he couldn't stop thinking about how she'd tasted when he kissed her.

They'd just reached the perimeter of the festivities when a shrill female gasp sounded a few feet away.

"Tana Thorpe? Is that really you?"

Chase's blood cooled at the sound of his ex-girlfriend's voice. Turning, he spotted the bride as she peeled away from her new groom and walked toward them, the skirt of her two-piece wedding gown billowing around her while the crop top showed off a band of bare skin. She'd dispensed with her bouquet of peach roses along with her pleasant veneer, openly scowling at Tana.

"Tana Blackstone, actually," Chase's date answered in a sweeter voice than he'd ever heard issue from her mouth. He almost did a double take, but managed to restrain himself while she extended a hand toward the other woman. "Congratulations on your marriage, Ashley."

Ashley Carmichael did not take Tana's hand. "Blackstone, of course. How could I forget the name of the woman who duped Chase?"

Ashley's gaze swept over him, still hostile after all these years. She was accustomed to having whatever—and whomever—she chose, so Chase's defection had wounded her pride.

He would have responded, but Tana seemed determined to keep the other woman's focus on her.

"I assure you my heart was broken far more than Chase's," Tana confided like they were longtime besties. "But that's so long in the past, and I want you to know you're one of the loveliest brides I've ever seen."

Surprise made Ashley's blue eyes track back and forth between them, clearly wary. But in the end, she patted the blond updo at the back of her head, where it had been interwoven with tiny white flowers.

"The gown was custom-made for me," she informed them, apparently taking the compliment at face value. "I insisted on the three-dimensional floral embroidery in the bodice and the Chantilly lace in the skirt." She swayed a little, as if for effect, making the skirt layers shift around her legs.

Impatient and wanting to put the confrontation with her father behind him, Chase was about to ask after him when Tana murmured encouraging comments about the gown.

"It suits you perfectly. I love the big bow tied with the excess fabric on the back of the bodice." Tana turned her melting-chocolate eyes up to him, smiling as she laid her left hand on his shoulder in a way that put her engagement ring on display. "I only hope my gown is half as pretty when Chase and I get married."

The bride's silence was so pronounced he had no choice but to shift his attention away from Tana to observe the other woman. Ashley's face had gone pale, her lips set in a hard, thin line.

"You have some nerve, Chase Serrano." The bride skewered him with one look, her raised voice attracting some attention from other members of the bridal party still posing for photos in front of a split rail fence along the edge of a picturesque field. "You're going to marry *her*?"

Her tone was so openly venomous Chase found himself wrapping a protective arm around Tana.

"I am. Thanks again for inviting us, Ashley. We'll let you return to your other guests." Without waiting for an answer, he tugged Tana away, hurrying her into the dim interior of the barn.

Peach and white roses clung to every surface.

Arrangements swathed the rafters, circled the free-standing candelabra, and wreathed the mounted elk's head over the huge stone fireplace. A fire was already burning in preparation for the cooling evening temperatures.

The band played in a far corner of the room, the dance floor empty save an older couple circling slowly. The sight of the white-haired pair, laughing at some private joke while they danced, gave Chase a pang over how lightly he'd been treating the idea of marriage.

"I'm ready for a performance critique." Tana stopped near the seating chart and ran an idle finger over the tables. She appeared lost in thought over the table arrangements while she prodded him in a low voice. "How did I do? Is that the kind of thing you were expecting?"

The down-to-business tone shouldn't have surprised him anymore since he'd long known about her efficiency and willingness to work hard. But after the way she'd maneuvered Ashley so effortlessly, he found it hard to believe she would require feedback.

"You were exceptional." Palming the small of her back through the silk dress, he guided her toward their seats at table twelve, a round one in the back of the room.

He felt her startle a bit as she peered up at him.

Was that disbelief he read in her eyes?

"What? You don't believe me?" he asked as they reached the spots with their place cards.

She set her purse and thin shawl on a chair, the

movement exposing an intricate crown and a small pair of wings tattooed between her shoulder blades. Unlike those he'd seen on her arms and neck before, this appeared permanent. When she straightened, the ink disappeared under her pink-streaked brown hair.

There was no point in taking a seat since the cocktail hour was still underway.

"I do. I'm just unaccustomed to words of approval." Lingering by the chair, she shrugged one shoulder in a gesture that appeared far from careless. "My dad perpetually found fault with me. I sold a character too hard, or I didn't sell it enough."

Anger leaped along Chase's nerves at the mention of the man, especially in this new context as antagonist to Tana.

"It hardly matters what a felon has to say about you or your talents," he bit out.

"When your father is the felon, it does. I may hate his crimes, but he was still the person who taught me how to make a peanut butter and jelly sandwich and tie my own shoes since my mother lacked any maternal instincts." Tana gave another awkward shrug, her delicate clavicle tilting with the movement and drawing his attention to the expanse of flawless skin above the bodice of her strapless gown. "Should we go take a photo in front of the rose wall?"

He recognized her obvious attempt to change the topic, yet he was inclined to let it pass until he had more time to mull over her difficult relationship with her family.

Whatever else might be an act with Tana, Chase

believed those mixed feelings were real enough. The fact that she'd avoided any trouble with the law in the years since he'd known her spoke of a commitment to a more honest life. And his private investigator corroborated the idea of Alicia Blackstone not having much use for her only daughter. The guy had found very little evidence of phone calls or visits between the pair.

"As you wish. You should send a photo to Sable so she can see you in that gown." He wouldn't mind a copy of the image himself, because he had the feeling once Tana signed over the piece of land to him, she would do her best to vanish from his life.

Of course, he would need her help for one more weekend.

His fingers shifted on her back as he walked with her toward the backdrop of flowers arranged for commemorative photos of the day, his fingers slipping lower to curve around her hip before he remembered himself.

How oddly natural it felt to touch her. To pull her close.

Her words from yesterday had played in an endless loop when he'd closed his eyes to go to sleep last night.

Please hurry up.

No doubt she'd craved that kiss as much as him. And yet she'd been the one to pull away, as if she'd recalled some pressing reason why they couldn't indulge the attraction. He'd give his left arm to know what that was.

Now, waiting in a short line of couples who would pose in front of the floral wall beneath an elk antler archway, Chase used the time to get to know her better. The more he understood her, the better chance he had of getting past her boundaries. So that the next time he kissed her, she wouldn't want to pull away.

"I have a question for you." Angling toward her, he spoke the words into the top of her hair as they stood side by side. He hadn't let her go yet, more than content to hold her against him under the pretext of their engagement.

"That sounds ominous." She peered up at him. "Anytime you preface a question with a warning, it can't be good."

The lavishly decorated barn was filling with more guests, and the country band began playing more upbeat tunes. The older dancing couple gave way to a handful of two-stepping pairs. Chase made a mental note to ask Tana to dance since the need to have her in his arms that way simmered like a fever in his blood.

"You mentioned you don't play cards anymore," he began, shifting his head lower, so it remained close to her ear. "May I ask why not?"

He'd watched her play a few hands with his friends at a long-ago party and had been mesmerized by the way she handled the cards. No doubt that should have been a clue about her past. But after taking the first few hands, she'd folded early and walked away from the game. She hadn't even taken her winnings, which had caused a bit of a stir among the group, even though they'd only been playing for imported beers.

"How can you question why?" Frowning up at him, she folded her arms in a defiant position. "I told you I left that life behind, Chase. I never ran scams for the love of it. It was the family business, and I would have been abandoned to foster care or sent to juvie if I didn't comply."

He couldn't miss the tension vibrating through her words. He felt it humming in her skin like electricity.

Should he believe her? Even as he framed the thought in his mind, he knew that he did. She'd been a convenient scapegoat when her father left the country, especially when Chase had felt far more personally betrayed by her. Or, if he were being completely honest, he'd felt foolish about falling for her.

"I'm sorry." He flagged down a waiter passing by with a tray of champagne flutes and took two, handing one to Tana. "I've spent so much time thinking about the wrongs that were done to me, I never considered how difficult it might have been for you."

Her arms relaxed as she accepted the drink, though her gaze remained wary as she lifted the glass to her lips and took a small sip.

"I was fed, clothed and loved—after a fashion. The moral compass I was given was obviously faulty, but I've worked hard to correct it. That's why I don't play cards anymore." She took another sip as they moved ahead in the line of people waiting for a photo.

The couple in front of them finished their pictures, and an attendant who managed the cameras waved Chase and Tana forward. They set their drinks on a table for that purpose, and for a moment, the activity gave him a chance to consider her words. Consider *her*. Tana Blackstone had surprised him in every possible way since he'd found her in Brooklyn Bridge Park. She was a different woman from the one he'd known eight years ago. Prickly and wary, yes. But also thoughtful and compassionate. She'd put effort into reforming her life once she'd left Nevada, and she'd done it without any help from her crooked family.

There was a lot to admire in that.

So as they wrapped their arms around each other for a photo in front of the peach and cream-colored roses, Chase allowed himself to simply enjoy the feel of her against his body. She was petite but fierce. She brandished her strength of character the same way she liked to flash the decorative spikes she favored.

And he was beginning to feel a few pangs of regret that he'd roped her into his plans for revenge. Especially when the next phase involved asking Tana to return to the poker table one last time.

After they finished their photo, the attendant encouraged them to input their email addresses on a small device so the images would be sent to them. Once they finished, Chase drew Tana toward their table again, but he took the long route behind one of the eight-foot-tall candelabra so he could say one more thing to her privately before they took their seats.

"For what it's worth, it's obvious to me that you've

put a lot of distance between yourself and your family." He finished his champagne in a long swallow and set aside the glass to direct his full attention on her.

The surprised expression on her face made him all the more sorry that he hadn't told her sooner.

"You don't have to say that. I'm going to help you secure your land either way." The candlelight made her pale skin glow, bringing out the hint of a flush in her cheeks.

"I wouldn't say it if I didn't mean it," he said simply. "I wish I hadn't—"

Chase stopped himself abruptly as he glimpsed a gray-haired man in a flashy tuxedo rushing toward them, his hand-tooled leather boots clomping loudly across the barn floor.

"What is it?" Tana glanced over her shoulder, no doubt to see what had claimed his regard.

Wariness strained his shoulders, and he curled a steadying arm around the woman next to him.

"Brace yourself. Our host looks like he's coming over to greet us personally."

Six

Tana may have leaned into Chase's strength a little. How could she not take comfort from him when the father of the bride was stalking toward them, nostrils flaring like a charging bull?

Built like a boxer with a square face and thick neck, Warren Carmichael appeared out of sync with the ranching way of life. Tana couldn't envision him working his land with his scrupulously slicked-back hair and pale skin that didn't see much sun. His tuxedo and leather boots were both decorative to the point of being almost fussy. He wore a rodeo buckle beneath his open jacket, yet he sported cufflinks on a shirt that looked custom tailored.

Tana, who'd never shaken the habit of sizing up

people quickly, pegged him as someone you didn't want to cross.

Their host raised his voice to be heard even before he reached them. "When Ashley told me who you'd brought here tonight as your guest, I had to come see for myself."

Dark, beady eyes fixed on her, and a chill shivered over her skin.

"This is the same girl who turned your head away from my Ashley?" he continued, coming to an abrupt stop just inches from her while the wedding party started to file into the barn from outdoors to find their seats.

People were bound to overhear.

"I'm Tana Blackstone, and I'm twenty-six, Mr. Carmichael. Hardly a girl." Tana offered him her hand to shake. "You have a beautiful home."

The man, like his daughter earlier, ignored the friendly offering. Instead, he swung his head toward Chase.

"She's the landowner, isn't she?" He jutted his chin, everything about his posture aggressive. "I spent a small fortune to find out who was behind that trust, but you knew all along, didn't you?"

For a moment, Chase imagined what Warren would have done with that information if he'd discovered the truth first. Would he have confronted Tana? Attempted to trick her into signing over the land to him?

Could he have gone so far as to threaten her? Just

the possibility made Chase want to rake the vision out of his eyes.

"No need to make a scene, Warren," Chase admonished the other man, trying to hold on to his cool. "You wouldn't want to upstage the bride on her special day."

The man frowned, but he did take a step back, the thought of upsetting his daughter clearly making an impact. For a moment, Tana couldn't help but think of her own father, who'd never felt protective of her. She'd simply been a useful tool in his scamming operations.

"The police might be interested to know that she's had it all this time." Warren spoke to Chase, but he eyed her. "She got off without any charges eight years ago, but if she benefited from her father's scam—"

"She didn't." Chase's arm was like an iron band around her waist, as if he wanted to be sure his enemy couldn't wrench her away.

It felt oddly comforting. She warmed where he touched her. And perhaps somewhat at his defense of her as well, even if he was just playing a role.

Still, the old guilt about her family returned, a heavy weight on her shoulders that felt all too familiar. She'd tried so hard to put the past behind her, but how could she when there were so many people still reeling from the consequences of her dad's schemes? How could she not blame herself for failing to turn him in sooner?

"According to her, maybe," the rich rancher

scoffed. "But these Blackstones make a living off of being good liars."

The confrontation was attracting attention now that more of the wedding guests were taking their seats. Heads swiveled toward her and Chase while Warren Carmichael steamed.

Still, Chase's touch anchored her through the encounter, his heat and strength both communicating that—in this, at least—he was on her side. That she was in no danger. It was a small thing, perhaps, but she'd been left to wriggle out of risky situations enough times on her own that she could appreciate having someone stand by her.

"I'll thank you to keep a civil tongue in your head in regard to my future wife," Chase answered quietly, lifting her left hand to kiss just above the knuckles. The gesture made her engagement ring catch the glow of the closest candelabra, sending rainbow fractals dancing.

If the Carmichael patriarch had been angry before, he grew livid now. His face flushed dark red. He pushed one finger against Chase's chest, ignoring her completely.

"Your wife? In other words, you're locking down that property either way through marriage. You son of a—"

"We're leaving," Chase announced, cutting the man off as he pushed aside the offending finger. "Give Ashley our best."

Leaving? Before they even took their seats for the

meal, when this event had been their whole reason for this charade?

Too surprised to know how to react, Tana was glad that Chase retrieved her bag and shawl for her before he led her toward the barn doors. The room had grown quiet, the argument having attracted all eyes by this time.

Gripping her short train in one hand to make walking easier, she hurried to keep pace with Chase's long stride. She held on to his upper arm, the muscle thick and hard beneath his jacket. She could hardly complain that they were leaving an event she'd wanted no part of from the beginning. Yet that relief was tempered by a growing awareness that this had likely been Chase's goal all along—to create a spectacle with his enemy and put the other man on alert about the land. In public. There were easily a hundred witnesses to the altercation.

Every bit of her training as a con artist told her that scene had been carefully choreographed for someone's benefit.

Warren Carmichael's? Or was Chase trying to hook someone else? And for what reason?

By the time they reached the valet stand and stepped into the back of their hired vehicle, Tana had a whole lot of questions simmering, ready for Chase to answer.

"Are you pleased with how that went?" She flipped the silk train free so it pooled on the floorboards near her feet.

No matter that she'd protested to Chase about the

wardrobe being too precious, there was no denying every gown was stunning. When she'd been a girl, her parents had used her wide-eyed, fragile looks to help rope in marks. So after she'd moved to New York and claimed her life as her own, she'd gravitated toward anything that might make her look like a gang member. Superficial as it sounded, people responded to those clothes. They were more wary around someone wreathed in leather and spikes.

Which was exactly what Tana wanted. No one could accuse her of tricking them if she never let anyone too close to her in the first place. The clothes were a first line of defense. Her costume. But she couldn't deny this ultrafeminine gown was beautiful to look at, and it made her feel beautiful to wear it. She just needed to be careful that she didn't start believing the message the dress sent out. Because she wasn't fragile.

And she was far from innocent.

Chase leaned back in the seat beside her while the hired car headed toward Cloverfield Ranch. "I'm very pleased with how it went. I assume you didn't mind leaving early?"

"Of course not. I just wish you'd told me that you wanted to make a scene. I might have been more willing to participate."

"We hardly crashed it." He frowned, as if he hadn't thought about it that way. "They'll go on to have dinner and dancing, with free drinks all night."

"And they will be talking about us the whole time, speculating on the argument and starting new rumors." She traced the outline of one of the pink roses on her skirt. "If you would share your endgame with me, maybe I'd be more help in whatever con you're running."

Chase double-checked the partition that separated the back seat from the driver of the chauffeured Land Rover. The return drive to Cloverfield was short enough, but who knew how much more provocative the conversation might get from here? Thankfully, the tinted glass had been fully raised. Chase preferred not to have the residents of this small ranching community gossiping about this conversation.

"Fooling people into thinking we're engaged isn't a con game. It's a simple deception. Misdirection." He spat out the last word with particular bitterness, recalling how easily he'd been misdirected from Joe Blackstone's real intentions toward Cloverfield Ranch.

"You're fooling people with a purpose. Intention." She stabbed a fingernail into the leather seat between them as they turned onto the main road. "I'm asking you to share it with me. Don't I deserve that much for flying out here to be a part of this charade in the first place?"

As she spoke, a tendril of pink-tipped hair slid forward in front of her shoulder, calling to his fingers. He tightened his hands into fists to avoid the temptation to test the texture and see if it was as soft as he remembered.

He'd been hard-pressed the night before to stay

away from her, knowing she was under his roof. He hadn't joined her for dinner or riding after that kiss they'd shared, certain he was too keyed up to keep things platonic. The fact was, he wanted her with an urgency he hadn't experienced in any of the eight years that had passed since they'd first met.

"I'm not sure," he answered carefully, watching the foothills of the Humboldt Range flash past the windows while they headed toward Cloverfield Ranch. "I thought I deserved your help after the role you played in the scheme to defraud my family. I don't know that I owe you any explanations."

She cast her gaze heavenward. Not a full eye roll, but close.

"Suit yourself. If you feel comfortable dragging me back to Nevada to expose me to the unreasonable anger of a man I've never even met before, then I will trust your judgment. But the sooner I can sign your papers and go home, the better." She leaned forward in her seat, as if she would leap from the vehicle as soon as the car stopped in front of the ranch house.

Seeing the tension thrumming through her, visible in everything from her stiff shoulders to the death grip on her clutch purse, Chase felt another pang of regret about what he'd asked of her. He hadn't anticipated the level of Warren Carmichael's fury, and he sure hadn't wanted it directed toward Tana.

"I hope you know I would never allow him anywhere near you." He had no choice but to reach for her, his hand falling on the soft skin of her upper back. She deserved his reassurance, even if he found it nearly impossible not to pull her closer. "That really was one of my primary goals in the engagement. Warren Carmichael hates me. But he won't threaten you if he thinks we're together."

The rigid set of her body eased a fraction. She glanced at him over her shoulder.

"You won't be there to stand guard once I'm back in New York." Her dark eyes held his for a moment before sliding away again. "I'm just hoping that signing over those lands ends whatever enmity he has toward me."

Unease troubled his conscience since he needed her to extend her fiancée role just a bit longer after the weekend ended.

She must have read the conflict in his features because she rounded on him as the hired car halted in front of Cloverfield Ranch.

"What? Does Warren Carmichael pose a threat I should be aware of?" The concern in her eyes—worry he'd put there—was a call to action to his scruples.

"Let's talk about it while we ride." He could tell he'd caught her off guard by the way her eyebrows shot up. "We have bonus free time since we didn't stay for the reception. We can talk on horseback."

How many afternoons had they ridden together that memorable summer? She'd loved being on horseback, and he'd loved seeing her there. Knowing that he'd introduced her to something that brought her joy had filled his chest with pride—up until he'd found out about her father's schemes.

Now he wondered if he'd overestimated the role she played back then. Either way, the desire to be with her that way again—riding side by side instead of the verbal sparring—was almost all-consuming.

"All right. I'll go riding with you." She allowed him to exit the vehicle and help her from it. They stood together on the stone walkway that led to the historic main house. "But I expect answers this time, Chase. I want to know the undercurrents between you and Warren, and why he's angry with me."

He nodded, knowing what she asked was both fair and reasonable. Also, he would have agreed to most anything to have this time with her on horseback again. It felt so right he could almost believe that all of his plotting and scheming to find her again and return her to Nevada had been to arrange this moment.

Of course it wasn't. But being with her here again felt that inevitable.

"I'll tell you everything. Can you meet me at the stables in fifteen minutes?"

"Certainly. As an actress, I can do a costume change in sixty seconds when I have to." She pivoted on one pink heel, her train trailing behind her, and headed into the house.

An hour later, Tana was dressed in jeans and boots once again and seated on a sorrel mare named Shasta. Beside her, Chase rode a tall buckskin gelding called Harley as they threaded their way through the foothills of the Humboldt Range. It had been unnerving to see how quickly she'd fallen into their old rhythms of readying their mounts. He'd led the animals to the crossties while she'd gathered tack. He'd helped her with the saddles even though she'd been managing just fine on her own. And when it was time to mount, he'd held her stirrup for her.

Such a small thing. Just twisting the metal ring so she had a better angle to mount.

And it had catapulted her backward like her own personal time machine.

Even now that they'd been riding for at least a quarter of an hour, she couldn't quite shake the mingling of past and present. How many times had they ridden this way, talking and laughing, sharing their dreams?

And if they found their rhythm together so easily on horseback, how quickly might they fall into sync in bed? The idea caused a shiver before she shut it down.

Those thoughts were foolishness. Distractions from her real mission here, which was to find out what Chase was planning, how it involved her and how she could settle the debt she owed him so she could walk away guilt-free.

She was about to begin an interrogation to that effect when he spoke first.

"I'd never guess you hadn't ridden in eight years." He glanced over at her as they kept a slow pace through a steep section of their old riding path. "You took to it again easily enough."

"You were a good teacher," she told him honestly. "Plus riding was a joy for me."

An escape. For those hours she was with Chase, she could almost forget her roots. Forget the fear that her father might be planning a scheme that could shake the foundations right out from under Chase and his mother.

She'd been so naive. So hopeful that she was free from her dad's scams for good.

"Did you take any of the horses out yesterday?" He shifted in the saddle to avoid a low-hanging branch on his side of the path. The trees were still sparse this close to the ranch, but they would become more numerous the higher they climbed.

"I did not. I realize I could have asked for a recommendation from one of the hands for which animal to saddle, but—" It wouldn't have felt the same without Chase. "I was tired."

She kept her focus on the path ahead, afraid her eyes would give away her real thoughts. Something stirred inside her the longer she spent with this man. Something she'd been sure was long dead.

"All the more reason I'm glad we escaped the wedding reception early, then. How are you liking Shasta?"

Tana bent over the mare's neck to stroke her, murmuring encouraging words to the animal. "She's perfect."

She felt the weight of Chase's gaze on her, but still couldn't bring herself to meet his eyes. The familiarity of this ride was breaking down her barriers faster than she could rearm herself.

"So, I promised you answers about Warren Carmichael," Chase began, catching her off guard with the abrupt shift in conversation. "I wasn't sure how much you knew about your father's relationship with him and was waiting to see how the two of you reacted to each other today. But it seems obvious to me now that you've never met him."

She swung on him, all her attention narrowing to this new twist in her understanding of the past.

"Never. And I had no idea Dad spent time with Ashley's father." Her mind raced, searching for memories of that summer. "Between how much time you and I spent together and how often my dad took trips to see my mother in Las Vegas—"

She cut herself off, realizing her misconception. Her mother had taken a condo close to the Strip that summer, and Tana had been under the impression her mom was spearheading the bigger con. Tana thought maybe her dad was providing support somehow by keeping himself away from her, when all along it was her father who had lured the bigger mark. That summer had been the beginning of the end to their marriage, though Tana hadn't realized it at the time. After Joe Blackstone disappeared, Alicia Blackstone moved on without a second glance back at her ex-husband or her daughter, either. Tana had honored her mom's self-imposed solitude in Las Vegas, especially after her mother remarried and hadn't even invited Tana to the wedding.

Chase waited a moment for her to continue, their mounts picking their way along the narrowing path.

When Tana didn't say anything more, Chase spoke again.

"Maybe he didn't take as many trips to Vegas as you thought. He organized some high-stakes local poker games, reeling in wealthy visitors to Warren's ranch. And, of course, Warren himself."

Missing pieces of an old puzzle fell rapidly together. Her father hadn't simply been conning Chase's mom while he'd been living at Cloverfield. He'd put his card sharp skills to work on the side, luring players to the table with higher and higher stakes, letting them feel comfortable that they could beat him, until the bets turned huge. That's when her father had struck, his true poker prowess coming out to beat the others when it counted.

"Dad took Warren deep. That's why Ashley's father holds a grudge." Her knee brushed against Chase's as their mounts shifted for room on the trail.

Awareness of him tripped through her veins. Involuntarily, she tightened her hold on Shasta's reins before forcing herself to relax again.

"Afterward, Carmichael told anyone who would listen that Joe Blackstone was a cheat. It was the only way he could save face in front of his friends who also lost a lot of money to your dad." At a fork in the trail, Chase steered his horse to the left, a route that opened up to a wide meadow between the hills.

Grateful for the sway of Shasta's steps that soothed her fraying nerves, Tana couldn't help filtering Chase's words through what she knew of her father since she'd spent all her formative years being party to his schemes. More often than not, her dad didn't cheat to win at cards. He had a keen intellect for the game and a natural feel for it that could have made him a ranked player if he chose to pursue the tournament route.

She'd suggested it to him more than once, never understanding why he'd turn down a legitimate way of making money. Her dad had tried to explain that it wasn't about money for him. It was about the thrill of the win. The rush that came from a successful con.

"That explains why Warren Carmichael hates my father. But I'm not sure I understand what he has against me." Her face burned at the memory of the man calling her out in front of a reception hall full of wedding guests.

"You know that land your dad put in a trust for you?" Chase asked, slowing Harley's pace until the horse stopped in his tracks.

Tana followed suit, reining in Shasta beneath the shade of a juniper tree.

"The one I'm signing over to you? Of course." She would have already done it if Chase had given her the paperwork. Settling the issue with that land was the main reason she'd traveled to Nevada.

"Apparently that plot isn't made up solely of lands that used to be in the Cloverfield Ranch parcel." Chase's gray eyes locked on hers, his voice stirring her senses even as she feared the rest of what he would say. "There are forty prime acres with river access that belonged to Warren Carmichael before your dad won them in a hand of poker."

Anger and resentment churned as this latest revelation rattled through her. Her father was at fault, without question. But didn't Warren Carmichael have some accountability for the loss, too? He'd gambled.

"There's my answer," she returned tightly, knowing that the joy of the ride was gone for the day. "Now it just remains for me to know if you want me to sign over that portion of the land to you, too? Or should I make restitution to Warren Carmichael for being foolish enough to bet his property?"

Too agitated to wait for his response, Tana nudged her horse forward. Breaking into a run, Shasta seemed as eager to put the conversation behind her as Tana was.

Still, as hard as the horse's hooves pounded the burnished meadow grasses, Tana knew they wouldn't outrun the trouble brewing.

Seven

Keeping his horse at an easy walk, Chase watched Tana's figure grow smaller in the distance, understanding she needed space.

For now, at least.

Hell, he didn't blame her for wanting to run from him. He'd deliberately blindsided her with the wedding and the meeting with Warren Carmichael, needing to see her reaction firsthand. He'd wanted to gauge for himself how much she knew about her father's side-hustle activities while he'd been in Nevada.

Having witnessed her surprise and confusion, Chase now believed she knew nothing about the poker games her dad had organized. The realization weighed uncomfortably on his shoulders, making him wonder what else he'd misjudged about her.

Tipping his head back, Chase watched a turkey vulture circling low overhead, silently riding the dry late-summer wind. He forced himself to take a deep breath and reconsider what he knew about Tana's part in her father's shady dealings.

Was it possible she hadn't known her dad had come to town to scam Chase's mom?

A week ago, he would have laughed at the idea. But considering her surprise about the trust her father had set up, and how readily she'd agreed to sign over the lands to Chase, he was beginning to question his former assumptions. Hadn't she tried to warn him not to trust her dad?

She'd been emphatic about that, but at the time, he'd thought she worried too much and had dismissed her concerns out of hand. That was on him.

Now, following the flight of the turkey vulture as it disappeared behind a rise, Chase pinched the bridge of his nose to counteract the tension headache that had Tana's name written all over it. No matter what Tana knew or didn't know, he owed her more courtesy than he'd extended so far.

Right? Or was he making excuses for how much he wanted to touch her? Taste her?

The need for her hadn't abated a bit in the years they'd been apart. If anything, she intrigued him more than ever. So if there was any chance that she hadn't been part of the setup to defraud his mom, Chase would learn the truth.

Which was why, after giving Tana a few minutes

to run off her frustration, he nudged his mount faster to overtake her.

There was only one spot she would be heading for. One place they'd ridden to over and over again that summer together. She was too smart a rider to venture anyplace but a well-known destination.

And yeah, thinking about the things they'd done in the remote privacy of that old cabin already had his blood simmering in his veins. Was she remembering them, too?

Minutes later, the original homestead on the historic Cloverfield Ranch came into view. A small wooden structure with a humbly stacked stone chimney, the building had long been abandoned as a residence, but it made for a good hunting cabin. Shasta stood nearby, grazing in the shade along a shallow creek bed.

At first, he didn't see Tana. But a moment later, as he guided Harley closer to the mare, he spotted her on the other side of the creek. She sat with her back against the smooth gray bark of a mountain alder tree, fingers sifting through some fallen leaves before pulling out a flat rock.

She must have heard him approach, yet she said nothing as she skimmed the stone along the surface of the creek water, being careful to aim away from where the horses were tied.

He allowed himself a moment to drink in the sight of her there in a place full of happy memories that all contained her. They'd had bonfires here, sharing their dreams over a stolen beer or two. They'd danced in the moonlight. He'd kissed her against the very tree where she now sat.

Then, of course, inside the shelter of that cabin, he'd discovered endless ways to give her pleasure. His entire sexual education had happened with her. No one else had quite measured up to her, and he needed to find out if he had some sort of euphoric recall. If he could just be with her again, maybe he could loosen the bond of the memories of the past. Then he could move forward.

Just thinking about the possibility tantalized him now as he slid off his mount and ground-tied his horse.

"You found your way back here." He made the obvious observation as he crossed the creek on a series of jutting rocks, his brain too full of hot memories to attempt more thoughtful conversation.

She glanced up at him, the pink tips of her brown hair brushing along the logo for her theater company emblazoned on her black T-shirt. She wore faded jeans today with no holes and no fishnet stockings beneath them. Even her black boots were practical. Not a stud or spike in sight.

Because she felt more comfortable here, back at Cloverfield Ranch with him? He dismissed the idea as soon as it formed, knowing that couldn't be the case. She'd just dressed for expediency. End of story.

"I took the only trail I remembered." She sifted through pine needles and came up with another stone. She studied it for a moment before tossing it with a side-arm throw. "We rode this way often enough."

His steps slowed as he neared her, his heart thudding heavily at the mention of what they'd shared here.

"Yes, we did." His voice deepened, his blood firing hotter.

Memories of their kiss the night before returned with a vengeance. She'd poured all of herself into that kiss up until the second she'd pulled away. He'd felt the heat. The passion. She'd singed his senses then, and every moment that they'd been together since then.

Now her dark gaze flickered up to his, latching on to it and holding steady.

"You said last night that we didn't have to fake the sparks between us." Her voice sounded as thick with desire as his. Unsteadily, she laid one hand against the alder tree and pushed herself to stand. "That attraction came naturally enough."

Even in the deep shade of the tree, he could see the leap of heat reflected in her eyes.

"I remember." His hands ached to touch her. Pull her close. Relive a thousand memories. "I said as much right after the kiss you ended."

He emphasized that last part, needing to remind her.

"Did you mean it?" Her gaze narrowed, almost as if she could ferret out his secrets if she studied him long enough. "That is, are you still attracted? Even now?"

"Hell, yes." How could she doubt it? Soon enough, she'd see for herself. "Come closer and I'll prove it."

She reached to tuck a strand of hair behind her ear, but he was pretty sure she did it to hide a shiver of desire. Her fingers had trembled for an instant.

"I only ended the kiss because I was afraid—" She jammed her hands into her pockets, hissing out a frustrated sigh. "I didn't like the idea of being the only one still feeling some of the old…feelings."

The admission surprised him. Although maybe it shouldn't, since her boldness was something he'd always admired about her. She spoke her mind and went after what she wanted. But then again, maybe she was only referring to attraction when she referred to the old emotions. Probably so.

He didn't want to mislead her by implying they were dealing with more than just physical desire. But then again, wasn't he experiencing a whole lot that wasn't precisely about sex?

He shut that thought down fast.

"You're not alone in any of that." He answered without considering the wisdom of honesty. He only knew he wasn't letting this moment get away from him if there was any chance Tana wanted the same thing as him. "Believe me, attraction wasn't on my personal agenda when I looked you up again. But here we are."

She gave a slow nod as the birds overhead chirped a cheerful chorus. "Here we are."

He waited, taking her measure in the swirling heat between them, not wishing to spook her.

Finally, he edged closer. Close enough to breathe in the clean scent of her skin. Close enough to track the patterns of light and shadow in her face from the sunlight filtering through the trees.

"Now that you know the sparks are one hundred percent mutual, what would you think about trying another kiss?"

The small stand of nearby trees seemed to lean in to hear her answer, the entire clearing holding its breath with anticipation. Only the creek babbled on, and one of the horses snuffled on the other side of the stream.

"I'd like that, Chase." Her chin notched higher, pupils widening with heat. "But you should know I won't be the one to end this one."

Tana knew she'd raised the stakes too soon.

If this had been a poker game, you didn't do that unless you were confident in your hand. And did she have any reason to be confident in what was happening between her and Chase? No. None.

But her father had always told her that her biggest weakness at the poker table was her lack of appreciation for measuring the odds ahead of time and working out all the probabilities.

Even realizing she was guilty of that same mistake now, Tana couldn't find it in her heart to care about the consequences. Not when Chase stepped so close his feet bracketed hers. His big hands clasped her waist, warming her skin right through the cotton of her T-shirt. His gray eyes seemed to see past all her smoke and mirrors to the woman she was beneath.

He knew her past. All the worst parts of her.

Yet somehow, miraculously, he seemed to want her every bit as much as she still craved him.

"I won't be ending this kiss, either," he promised, the words wrapping around her more seductively than any embrace. "Not unless you tell me to."

Her heart pounded so loudly he must have heard it. The sound filled her ears even as her fingers walked up his chest to rest on his broad shoulders. "Do your worst, cowboy."

In spite of her taunting, Chase brushed the softest of kisses over her lips. Testing. Teasing.

Her bravado melted underneath the skillful seduction, her whole world narrowing to the play of his mouth over hers. Nipping. Licking. Sucking.

Every stroke of his tongue stoked the fire inside her, making her ache and squirm in his arms, desperate for more. For everything. Especially since she could feel the rock-hard length of him pressing against her belly.

Edging back, she gasped his name.

"Chase. Please." She cupped his bristled jaw in her hand, her fingers tracing his cheekbone. "I need more."

His growl of satisfaction rumbled right through her. "Me, too. Are you okay with the cabin?"

A thrill shot through her at the prospect. This was happening. Her and Chase Serrano. After all these years.

Despite all the reasons that it was probably a really bad idea, Tana couldn't wait another minute.

"You could take me against this tree, and I'd ask for more."

His gray eyes went molten silver.

"Don't tempt me." He spun on his heel and led her toward the cabin, his long strides necessitating that she double-step through the dried pine needles and fallen leaves.

If she wasn't so thoroughly turned on she might have laughed at the picture she must make, practically sprinting back to this man's bed in spite of everything that had happened between them.

Reaching the cabin, he nudged the door open and pulled her inside after him. Despite the rustic exterior, the interior was clean and well maintained, if sparsely furnished.

She guessed a cleaning crew must make regular rounds here since Chase didn't live in Nevada full-time. The scent of pine and lemon polish pervaded the space. They headed toward the lone bed, only breaking their kiss long enough for him to pry open the cupboard so he could reach past the linens and towels to withdraw a silky blanket and flannel sleeping bag.

A smile tugged at her lips as the past merged with the present. She'd forgotten that detail about being with him here in the past. They'd laid down a sleeping bag on the bed to explore one another's bodies, camping out here until just before dawn, then riding home, sweetly sore but well sated.

A surge of nostalgia threatened to haul her into the past where old hurts lay, so she purposely stomped it back down. Instead, she took the heavy flannel from him, needing an activity.

Her breasts brushed his arm as she moved, sending a jolt of electric heat through her.

"Here. I can help." She unzipped the insulated bag and laid it out on the queen-size mattress that took up almost the whole bedroom.

When she finished, she realized Chase had been watching her closely. Studying her, almost.

"You're nervous." It wasn't a question.

Her pulse sped faster as she smoothed the fabric over the bed. "It's been a long time since I—" She licked her lips. "Was with someone."

Years, actually.

She'd been with exactly two other people besides Chase. The first had been a disaster from start to finish, never to be repeated. The second had been a boyfriend she'd cared about, but the sex had never come close to what she remembered with Chase. Both of those had been a long time ago; her focus had been on work and not romance for the last few years.

Now Chase dropped the soft quilt he'd been carrying and wound his arms around her.

"Don't worry. It's like riding a horse." A wicked smile curved his lips. "You don't forget."

Welcome laughter bubbled freely from her, banishing her nerves.

"That's excellent news." She twined her arms

around his neck, arching her back so her hips met his. "Will you show me?"

The hungry sound that emerged from the back of his throat heightened her senses as the last of her reservations fell away.

"I've been thinking about little else since that kiss last night," he admitted before his mouth claimed hers.

She tipped her face up to his, offering him more. Everything.

Each stroke of his tongue drugged her, her knees turning liquid under her. Her hold on his neck tightened, his body the only thing anchoring her in a world going up in flames.

This was what she remembered. Fire. Passion. A connection so strong that she didn't have to think about how to proceed or worry about what he thought of her. They were too busy setting each other ablaze.

She tunneled her hands under his shirt, eager palms splaying over his abs to trace the ridges and valleys. The lean athletic frame of his youth had filled out to hard-muscled perfection.

She had to see for herself. Breaking the kiss, she lifted the tail of his shirt higher, then sucked in a breath at the sight of him. Jeans riding low on his hips, Chase had a body that was the stuff of fantasy. With a fingertip, she followed the valley along his obliques before dragging her knuckle along the denim waistband, his breathing growing harsh in her ear as she touched him.

Pausing at the button, she worked it free with

some effort, the fabric straining to contain him. She would have moved to the rest of the buttons, but he captured her hands in one of his.

"Let me." His voice rasped against her ear. "It's been too long for me, too. I'm not sure I have enough restraint to survive those fingers working me over like that."

Her gaze shifted to his as she tried to hide her surprise. She wouldn't have guessed this man of potent sexuality would take any downtime, assuming he must have his pick of women to bring home.

Still, the idea pleased her far more than it should. Why should she care who he slept with?

But Chase was already stripping off his jeans and stepping out of them, distracting her from her thoughts and putting all her focus right back on him. He peeled off his shirt next, leaving him wearing nothing besides his boxers.

"Oh." She reached for him again, but he sidestepped her, gathering her wrists in one hand.

"Your turn, Tana." He hooked a finger in the neckline of her T-shirt and tugged it lightly. "Do you want to do the undressing, or do you want me to?"

"Your hands would feel better than mine," she confessed, already yanking the hem of her shirt from her pants. "But I'll be faster."

She kept her eyes on him while she toed off her boots and shimmied out of her jeans. His gaze tracked her every movement, and the only sound was the old cabin creaking gently in the late-summer wind.

When she slid a bra strap off one shoulder, Chase stopped her, his hand curving, holding, caressing.

"Wait." He stepped closer, the warmth of his body heating hers even before they touched. "Efficiency be damned. I can't let you have all the fun."

When she released the black satin strap, Chase's fingers slid beneath it, grazing her shoulder. At the same time, his hips nudged hers, the impressive erection pressing into her belly.

Biting back a gasp, she felt her eyelids flutter closed, the better to concentrate on all the new sensations bombarding her.

"Chase." She hummed the name to herself, wanting to soak up everything he had to offer. His pine-and-musk scent. His heat.

His strength.

"I'm going to take the best care of you, Tana." He breathed the sensual promise in her ear. "Relax and let me."

The huff of his breath near her temple gave her goose bumps. She gripped his shoulders, balancing herself on her toes as she swayed still closer to him.

"Yes. I want you to." She didn't recognize her voice or the sentiment behind it. Since when did she hand over control to anyone? For any reason.

But she didn't want to worry about that now. She just held on tighter while he peeled down the satin fabric and exposed a nipple to the cool air. A moment later, he lowered his head to kiss her there, his tongue playing back and forth across the tight peak.

Pleasure rippled through her, her whole body hungry for more. She pressed her hips to him, seeking pressure. Needing him.

He understood, too. Because a moment later, he'd removed her bra and lifted her against him before laying her on the bed. She shivered at the sight of him looming over her. Ready for her.

Except…an unhappy thought occurred to her.

"I don't have condoms." She bolted upright, guessing Chase wouldn't be able to magically produce some from the small bathroom in the hunting cabin.

Provisions were limited here.

"I picked some up last night." Leaning down, he retrieved his jeans and pulled a foil packet from the pocket. "After that kiss, I figured it couldn't hurt to—"

She kissed him. Hard.

Grateful for the presumption that would let them be together. She didn't know how she'd gone from ignoring the unwise attraction last week to exploring every facet of it today, but she knew there was no turning back now. She needed this.

Him.

"You're a very smart man," she praised him, plucking the packet from his fingers to tear it open. "Thank you for this."

He watched her as he lowered his boxers. "You're not the only one who benefits, believe me."

Her heart rate quickened, her attention captivated. Distracted, she fumbled the condom, dropping it on the bed.

Luckily, Chase was ready to finish the job. He

rolled the prophylactic in place before gripping her thighs and dragging her to the edge of the bed to put her in the best position for...

"Oh. Chase." Tana wrapped her legs around his waist as he pressed his way inside her.

For a moment, they remained still. Locked together. Breathing each other in after so many years apart.

Then the heat began to build even before he moved. And when he did, easing partway out and entering her all over again, she almost wept at how good it felt. How good *he* felt.

She hadn't dreamed this. Hadn't inflated her sense of how amazing they'd been together. If anything, this was even better.

The realization both gratified and daunted her.

Sure, she'd been right, and that was nice. But Chase Serrano was only in her life very temporarily. So she needed to enjoy every second of this before he was gone again for good.

"Are you with me?" he asked, pausing to comb his fingers through her hair, sifting through the strands and kissing his way along her jaw. "You looked like you disappeared for a second."

"Just wondering how it could feel this way when we haven't seen each other in so long. When there's so much...unsettled between us." She regretted mentioning it as soon as she'd said the words.

Sex should be simple. Physical.

She had no wish to discuss the emotional side of their unorthodox, renewed relationship.

"I don't know." His voice was grave, his eyes never leaving hers as he reached between their bodies to stroke between her legs. "But you're welcome to stay in my bed until you have the answers you're looking for."

Her breath caught at the way he touched her, his fingers teasing her higher while he slid into her, again and again.

Heart pounding faster, she felt the orgasm building. Needed the release it offered. Her eyes closed while she let the sensations tighten and coil, ready to spring.

She was holding her breath, anticipating, when Chase spoke softly in her ear.

"Would you like that, Tana?"

Visions of lingering here, in bed with him, while they pleasured each other day and night only made her release hit harder. Sweet shock waves reverberated through her, blinding her to everything but what she was feeling.

She tightened her hold on his hips with her legs, her body arching hard into his.

She hadn't even come down from that high when she felt Chase still. When he found his own release, the pulsing of it pushed her toward a second orgasm, a brief, sweet shadow of the first.

It left her wrung out and spent, still wondering how she could have such an incredible connection to a man who didn't trust her. A man still withholding secrets of his own.

When he lay down beside her in the aftermath,

dragging the second blanket over their cooling bodies, Tana didn't know where to begin untangling all the messy emotions she had as far as Chase was concerned. For now, she just breathed in the scent of Chase and sex, telling herself she'd sign over the deed to the property tomorrow and fly home to Brooklyn.

Maybe then, back in the safe haven of her shared apartment building with her girlfriends, she'd be able to work through the complicated knot of everything she didn't want to feel.

But even as she burrowed into the crook of Chase's arms, she knew that was naive thinking. No matter how much they connected in bed, she had to remember that he'd requested a fake engagement with her for more than one reason. And she had the feeling he'd only just begun to reveal the depths of whatever revenge he had in mind for Tana.

Eight

Night had fallen before Chase convinced himself they needed to return to the main ranch house.

But damn, he still didn't want to leave the bed he shared with Tana. The last few hours with her in the cabin had been like stepping into the best part of his past, returning to a time when he hadn't thought of anything beyond her.

Of course, that had been foolish of him back then. He'd like to think he knew better now. This time, he could enjoy the incredible connection they shared without giving her his heart or his trust.

Moonlight shone through the thin glass windowpanes and onto the queen-size bed, the air beginning to cool now that the sun had set, since the old homestead had only a fireplace to regulate the temperature. The pale light illuminated Tana's face where she lay in profile facing him, her bare shoulders showing no evidence of the henna tattoos that had been there the day before. He didn't think they were easy to scrub off.

The thought provided just the excuse he needed to delay returning to the main ranch house for a few more minutes at least.

"I noticed the tattoos were gone today," he observed, grazing a fingertip along her collarbone and over her shoulder before trailing down one slender arm.

"All but one." She didn't glance up at him, her attention focused on tracing the plaid pattern in the flannel blanket beneath them.

"The crown and wings." He remembered seeing them on her back earlier.

Her finger stilled. She glanced up at him.

"Those are the only real ones I have. I don't mind them being permanent because I don't see them as often. But I like changing what I wear on my arms since I look at them every day." She returned to her idle tracing.

Deciding to circle back to the wings, he asked the other question that tugged at him.

"Where did you learn to draw like that? All the henna work was so detailed." If she'd possessed that kind of artistic talent when they'd known each other, she'd never shared it with him.

"Practice. Lots of practice." For a moment, it seemed as if that was all she'd say about it. But then she drew in a deep breath and continued. "I'm not sure how much you read about my family, but I was born in Flushing, Queens. Close to an Indian neighborhood."

He'd read everything he could find about her in those months after her father's scam. Then he'd learned even more from the private investigator who'd ultimately found her in Brooklyn. That had still left big gaps in his knowledge about her since her father had often used aliases that he'd shared with his wife and daughter.

"I remember. You left the city when you were still young." He'd read that her dad had run afoul of the Russian mob and moved to the West Coast. Tana would have been about ten years old.

She propped herself up on one elbow, giving him her full attention.

"Right. I was sad to go because it meant I had to leave the neighbor who'd been my sitter when my parents were...busy." A frown curved her lips before she spoke again. "Kalyani ran a beauty shop out of her apartment, and she was especially known for her henna work."

"She taught you?" He remembered how detailed Tana's drawings were with their elaborate shading and intricate designs.

"No. But I watched her work often enough. Sometimes brides would be there for eight hours while Kalyani applied the designs." She smiled to herself. "I'd beg her to draw on me, but she never did."

He waited, curious about her friend since Tana

had already spoken more about this woman than she ever had about her parents.

"But before I left Queens, she drew me a crown that she said belonged to Kali, a fierce protector goddess. Under the crown, she drew angel wings, and she told me those were for my guardian angel to keep me safe wherever I went." Her smile wobbled a little. "I'm sure she knew I would be facing a tougher life once I left her."

Chase nodded, understanding. "You started working more for your father after that."

"I felt I had no choice," she said shortly. Then her voice softened again as she continued. "Anyway, I saved the paper with her sketch for years. During college, I took the drawing to a tattoo parlor to have the design permanently inked."

Empathy for all she hadn't said—the dangers she'd faced under the roof of criminal parents—crowded his chest. Picturing her as a ten-year-old kid couldn't help but shift his perspective a bit. No way she'd chosen crime at that age.

"I'm sorry you didn't have a protector." He cupped her face in his palm, realizing this time with her was doing more than shift his perspective.

He was starting to care all over again.

The thought startled him so much his hand slid away from her cheek. Perhaps some of his dismay showed on his face because she reared away from him, levering up on her pillow.

"We should get back," she blurted suddenly, her eyes darting to look anywhere but at him.

Damn it.

Had he revealed his thoughts somehow? He blinked, as if that could help erase whatever had been reflected on his face or in his eyes.

"Tana—"

She shook her head, already scrambling off the bed. "I'll need time to shower before our meeting with the attorney and the notary."

He studied her a moment, wondering if he'd offended her. He pinched his temple, wishing he could rewind the last couple of minutes so that they could talk through things instead of retreating to their old standoff of mistrust. Could she blame him for not trusting her after the con her father pulled? She said she didn't have a choice. But why hadn't she turned to Chase for help if she really wanted to get out from under her family's thumb?

Why hadn't she chosen him?

But the moment for that conversation had passed, and maybe it was just as well. He had business to attend to.

"Right. My lawyer should be arriving at the ranch house soon with the documents to sign over the deed." Chase pushed off the bed to retrieve his clothes.

This wasn't how he'd wanted their time together to end, but then again, he hadn't thought beyond the need to be with her again. To see if the chemistry were still as potent as he'd remembered. Now that he knew it was even hotter? He didn't have any idea how to handle that. Tonight, he just needed to move forward with their paperwork and reclaim his lands.

That would at least finalize their business at Cloverfield. Later, he'd see about using their engagement to lure her father out of hiding.

Because no matter what feelings he was starting to have for Tana, Chase wouldn't abandon his plans for revenge on her father anytime soon.

Back at Cloverfield Ranch, Tana had retreated to her room as quickly as possible, needing some breathing room after what had happened between her and Chase.

Ducking into the lavish marble shower stall, she tried to wash away the fear that she'd made a huge mistake by sleeping with her host. Soaping her sensitized skin, she was torn between berating herself and reliving every single detail of their time together. In slow motion.

His touch had transported her back in time to the happiest summer of her life. His kiss had stirred all the same sensual energy, filling her with a heat that no other man had ever summoned.

It was unfair, given that he'd only wanted a fake engagement to further his own schemes. Schemes she didn't fully understand yet.

As she worked the citrus-scented shampoo into a lather, Tana thought back to the way Chase had set her up to confront Warren Carmichael. He'd said he wanted to see for himself if she knew Warren, apparently not trusting her word. But why was that

important to him? Did he think Warren and her father had colluded somehow to defraud Chase? She
knew nothing about the poker games her father had
organized while he'd lived in Nevada.

When her scrubbing didn't coax any answers to
the surface of her brain, she tipped her head into the
hot water designed to fall like a rain shower from the
ceiling as steam rolled up and around her. Somehow,
the poker games of her father's past were important
to Chase. But why would Chase care if her dad had
taken Warren Carmichael deep at the card table?

Chase had an agenda he hadn't shared with her
yet. Maybe he never would. The idea stung since
she already knew she would forever associate this
trip with the hours spent in his bed. No doubt it had
meant more to her than him. She'd read the retreat
in his expression during her misguided attempt to
share something about her past with him. He hadn't
wanted to get to know her beyond what they'd enjoyed physically.

Which was fine. She understood, even if there
had been a moment when she'd felt a twinge of hurt
at how fast he'd pulled away. Especially when she'd
tried to share something of herself with him. Something real.

But he wasn't interested in the woman beneath
her armor now any more than when they'd been in
their teens. He'd brought her here to play a role,
and she'd done that. Once she signed over the lands
to him, she would consider their fake engagement
over, and she'd never see Chase Serrano again. And

while the idea already hurt, Tana knew it was the only way to keep her heart safe.

Chase shouldn't have been surprised when Tana strutted into the library wearing the silver-studded high-top sneakers and ripped jeans with black tights under them. Her vintage Sex Pistols T-shirt would have cemented his understanding of her mood, but she'd taken it a step further by inserting a splashy green stud in her nose piercing and stenciling a henna snake on the back of her left hand.

If it had been just the two of them in the room, he might have laughed out loud at the way she'd drawn the snake's open jaws positioned around her engagement diamond, as if it were about to swallow the ring whole.

But Chase's attorney and a local notary were already seated at the walnut desk in the corner, their four chairs drawn around it to ease the signing process.

The notary, an older woman who worked at an area bank, appeared to hide a smirk as she peered over her half-glasses at Tana striding toward the group. Chase's lawyer, a friend from college, followed Tana's every movement with an interest he didn't disguise well enough for Chase's liking.

Maybe that was what drove Chase to his feet to meet her midway across the library floor. He couldn't help the need to loop a possessive arm around her.

Had it only been a couple of hours since he'd had

her naked beneath him? It already felt like years. And he needed her again.

Lowering his head to kiss her on the cheek, he had the chance to speak softly to her. "Was it something I said that brought on the wardrobe change?"

"I'm sure I don't know what you mean," she said in an innocent voice that borrowed heavily from her Blanche DuBois character.

Her clean, citrusy scent made him want to taste her. His hand tightened on her waist for a moment before he turned to the others.

"Sharon, Hunter, this is my fiancée, Tana Blackstone. Tana, meet Sharon Eckert and Hunter Randolph." Chase shot his lawyer a level gaze, making sure the guy got the message.

Or he would have, if Hunter had ever torn his attention from Tana.

Chase felt a scowl settle on his brow, but at least Hunter skipped small talk in favor of business, quickly explaining the paperwork as Chase and Tana took their seats. Knowing already what he was asking her to sign, Chase took the next few minutes to observe Tana more closely.

She looked as delectable in her jeans and tennis shoes as she did in the gown she'd worn to the wedding, her beauty transcending whatever she wore. Both those sides of her were so different from his favorite aspect of her, though: the simple, pared down woman who'd joined him on horseback.

For those hours at least, she hadn't bothered to hide behind a role.

And he'd been foolish enough to close the door on that tenuous connection he'd formed with her.

"Chase?"

His friend's voice called him out of his musing. He realized three sets of eyes were all turned his way. Clearly he'd missed something while he'd been contemplating Tana.

Her jaw tightened, full lips pursing.

"Sorry?" Leaning forward, Chase refocused on the task at hand.

Hunter slid a document across the polished wood surface of the desk. "Your fiancée would like to know if she'll be signing over the former Carmichael property to you in this deed. Did you explain to her how that works?"

Of course he hadn't. He'd been too busy undressing her.

Tasting her. Satisfying her the best way he knew how.

Judging from the daggers in her brown eyes right now, however, he realized he should have set aside time to do more than that this afternoon. But she'd been upset when she first learned that her father had won a parcel of land that had once belonged to Carmichael in a card game. Tana had ridden away from him and they'd never returned to that conversation, or the plans he had for that particular piece of land that Tana now owned. Chase didn't want her to sign that part of the property over to him.

He needed her to keep ownership of that portion of the parcel her father had put in trust for her. Temporarily, at least, until Chase had the chance to enact the rest of his plan for revenge.

"Hunter, Sharon, will you excuse us for a moment?" Chase didn't think either of them would mind since he was paying them well to make a house call on a Saturday.

And a moment later, he had Tana all to himself in the library. The door snicked closed behind the others as they departed, sealing Chase and Tana in privacy.

Before he could speak, however, she surged from her chair, slapping a hand on the desk as she stood.

"What the hell are you doing?"

Anger whipped through her as she stared into Chase's gray eyes.

Not just because he hadn't bothered to explain half of his schemes to her. Also because their time together had changed exactly nothing between them, and she was fast regretting giving her body to a man who couldn't bolt from her bed fast enough.

He had the audacity to nod, as if she'd made some obvious observation of little concern. "It's very simple, actually—"

"Don't." She pointed a finger at him, her abandoned chair rolling back. "You don't get to mansplain this to me now when you've been deliberately evasive all weekend about what I'm doing here."

"I didn't know how much I could trust you."

"That's why you took off my clothes rather than talk to me?" She shoved away from the desk to storm around the library, a book-laden man cave from another century.

The whole place screamed wealth, from the humidor holding some of the world's best cigars to the bottles of Macallan and Chivas on the bar cart. Rare old volumes graced the bookshelves. It was a world she'd seen many times while she'd been an unwilling part of her father's schemes. And she had no desire to return to it. Whatever she possessed now, she owned because of her hard work.

"That's not fair," Chase said quietly, still seated at his desk while she walked off some of her agitation. "I thought we both wanted to be there. Very much."

She pivoted to face him, needing to see his features to gauge his sincerity. He sat with fingers steepled, studying her. She held her silence, though, determined to wait him out.

"I will allow," he continued, "that I should have made time to discuss this with you in detail. But the chemistry that kicks in sometimes between us…you have to admit it's potent. Distracting." His brow knitted, as if he couldn't possibly account for their connection. "It threw me."

"Explain that to me," she demanded, not backing down now. "What do you mean it 'threw you'?" Her heart did a little leap at his words even as she told herself that was ridiculous.

More time with Chase could only lead to heartache and disaster when she *knew* he wanted vengeance on her family.

"Tana, you know perfectly what it means. You

were there with me. Today stirred old memories. For a little while, it felt like old times, and we both know that's dangerous terrain." His jaw muscle flexed. "You don't want to revisit the past any more than I do."

She bit back a half dozen retorts to that loaded statement.

"We're getting off track," she said finally, determined to finish signing the papers as soon as she understood the language of the documents that required her signature. "Just tell me what's happening with Warren Carmichael's land. Why isn't it included in the real estate transfer that I'm signing over to you?"

There'd been separate paperwork for those forty acres, and Chase's lawyer had told her not to sign it yet. Confused, she'd asked for clarification, and that had held up the whole meeting.

Did Chase want the land to be returned to the Carmichael family? She was fine with that, given that her father had obtained it in a card game. But she didn't understand why she couldn't sign and be done with it tonight.

What was Chase planning? What had he been hiding from her?

Rising from his seat, Chase came toward her. Each footstep made her heart race faster. She should not want him this much. But her body did not understand the message.

When he reached her, his hands slid around her elbows. His fingers pressing gently into the tender skin there. Amazing how an elbow could become an erogenous zone when Chase was involved.

"Warren wants that land badly. I'd like you to hold on to it to entice him into a high-stakes poker game next weekend at my house in the Hamptons."

Her heart sank to the floor. No, lower. Chase had far bigger schemes afoot than she'd ever guessed.

"I don't gamble." She hadn't touched cards since she turned eighteen.

She would not. Memories of past games—grown men losing their life savings on the turn of the cards—sickened her.

"You wouldn't be playing with your own money. You'd use the land as your buy-in." Chase's hands never left her. He touched her so gently when his words ate into her skin like acid.

"It doesn't matter. I. Don't. Play." Turning away from him, she folded her arms tight. How many times had she fought this battle with her father? And lost. He'd been an expert in coercion, using his manipulative tactics on his own daughter to ensure she kept dealing cards. Her gut roiled. "I told you I left that life for good, and I meant it."

"You left the con game. This isn't a con. It's a perfectly legal poker game, the same as they play in casinos all over the country."

"You sound exactly like my father." He'd made the same argument to her plenty of times.

If Chase took offense, he didn't show it. "I'm not asking you to do anything against the law, and you know it."

She thrust her hands over her head in exasperation. "So go find the closest riverboat with gaming tables and have a blast, but leave me out of it."

In the silence that followed, she heard the soft ticking of a grandfather clock, the moon chasing the sun across the sky on the antique face. Tana stared at it, wishing the sun would win soon so she could be back in Brooklyn where she belonged, far from Cloverfield Ranch and her father's misdeeds that wouldn't stop haunting her.

"I'm not good enough to beat him."

She shook her head, not sure how to argue the point. She couldn't take on Chase's plan for vengeance for him. Even if it wasn't illegal, it was still unethical to play a game with such stacked odds. And yes, she'd been an excellent player once upon a time. It had brought her no joy. Only pain.

After a long moment, Chase continued.

"I need to even the score with Warren for two reasons," he admitted, his gray eyes weary. "First, because he dragged me into a game right after my mother lost her land, telling me it was a chance to win something back." His voice had never sounded so bitter.

"Oh, Chase." She knew how that story ended. Emotional players never won. The cards didn't care if you were angry. Or desperate. If anything, they were all the crueler to people who were on the verge of losing everything. "How could he? And what did you even have left that he wanted?"

"A cash inheritance from my dad." He moved toward the bar cart, opened a heavy crystal decanter and poured two fingers' worth of dark amber liquid into a rocks glass. "Your father hadn't taken that from me. Just the land."

He downed half the drink while Tana's stomach knotted with a fresh pain. She'd thought she felt sick before. But this new development made her dizzy with anger.

Her dad might not have taken Chase's last savings directly, but he had stirred the fever for high-stakes poker in the area. That gambling fever led to the kind of game that must have lured Chase to risk his money.

"Bastard," she said softly, even though she knew her father was far worse than Warren. "I'm so sorry."

For a long moment, Chase said nothing. He sipped the second half of the drink more slowly while the clock ticked down their time together. Tomorrow they'd return to New York first thing in the morning. Although if Chase had his way, Tana would be seeing him in the Hamptons next weekend for a poker game.

Not that she'd be playing. Finally, when Chase didn't seem inclined to say anything more, Tana spoke. Dared to ask the question that circled around her head.

"What's the second reason you want to face Warren at the card table? You said there were two."

Setting his drink down, Chase faced her.

An unhappy premonition settled inside her, making her dread his next words.

"I think you already know." His level look chilled

her even before he continued. "A card game with an aggressive, reckless player like Warren Carmichael is sure to draw your father out of hiding."

Nine

Two days after returning to New York, Tana cursed the high heels she'd worn to today's afternoon audition. She'd managed to channel the pain of pinched toes into a kick-ass audition for a small role in a soap opera. But as she walked from the subway station back to her apartment, the blisters proved too much.

Every step lodged the back of her shoe deeper into the broken skin on her heel, a sting that wouldn't have hurt as much if she thought she had a snowball's chance of getting the soap opera part she'd tried out for. But she'd guessed from the high percentage of models at the casting call that the show was more interested in a pretty face than killer acting skills.

With *Streetcar* nearing the close of its four-week run, Tana was staring at potential unemployment again soon if she didn't nail a new acting gig. The prospect weighed heavily on her, as did her looming bills. Yet the stress of being jobless seemed like a dance party compared to the far greater stress of the poker game at Chase's house in Southampton slated for Saturday night. She knew he would be promoting the game up and down the eastern seaboard, hoping to draw her father out of hiding. She wasn't sure what upset her more about that. The possibility of facing her dad again after all these years? Or might there be some actual worry about her dad being arrested after all this time?

Of course not. She wanted justice for Chase. Her father deserved the jail time. But there were risks to an old con coming out of hiding. There were more dangerous enemies to Joe Blackstone than the police. And even after all his crimes, she didn't want him to be hurt.

Then, there were worries for herself, too. Eight years ago, her skills had been top-notch, even when she didn't cheat. But she wouldn't employ the old tricks anymore. Not when she'd striven so hard to live honestly since she'd turned eighteen.

It hurt that Chase had asked her to play. She hadn't realized until then how much she hoped he would see her differently now. See the woman she'd tried so hard to become. But she was only useful to him as a part of her old life. A crook's daughter.

"Ow. Ow. Ow." Hobbling up the steps to the brownstone, Tana could hear rock music vibrating through the front door as she approached.

Normally, the sounds of female laughter and electric guitar would have her smiling after a hard day, since it meant girl time with her favorite people in the world, Sable and Blair. But tonight she had the feeling her roomies were waiting to ambush her. Blair had cornered her multiple times since Tana returned home Sunday, bombarding her with questions about what had happened with Chase.

Tana's hand hovered on the front door handle. She wasn't sure if she was ready to face them.

A loud burst of laughter from inside made up her mind, however. She had friends—genuine, sweet friends—for the first time. She'd been so isolated growing up, never allowed to get attached to anyone since her family had moved so often. No way would she run from a chance to enjoy the bond with Sable and Blair.

Not when she desperately needed the counsel of wiser heads than hers. Hauling open the door, she called into the building.

"Honey, I'm home!" She yanked off her offending shoes and left them on the welcome mat. As much as she would have enjoyed hurling them across the room, she needed to take them to a consignment shop. Maybe she could get credit toward a better-fitting pair.

A happy squeal sounded from downstairs in the kitchen, accompanied by Blair's voice shouting, "You're just in time for Mont Blanc chocolate pavlova!"

The scent of chocolate and something nutty

floated up the sweeping mahogany staircase along with Blair's words.

"I have no idea what that is, but it smells amazing." Dropping her backpack on the marble console table, Tana hurried barefoot down the staircase connecting the entry-level parlor with the kitchen on the garden floor.

Inside the all-white kitchen, Sable sat on a granite countertop slathering whipped cream on a confection that looked like a meringue-covered cake on a layer of chocolate mousse while Blair finished washing a mixing bowl at the sink.

"Don't ask me what it is." Sable grinned up at Tana as she entered, pausing in her work to wink. She wore a pink T-shirt that said We're Hungry with a red graphic heart over her baby bump. "I just co-opted the frosting duty so I could lick the spoon."

"Guys, come on. Don't you watch any baking shows?" Blair asked, blond ponytail swinging as she opened a cabinet to pull out glasses, setting three on the white-and-gray-flecked granite. "A pavlova is a meringue-based dessert, and I made this one chocolate. And the Mont Blanc part refers to the chestnut puree topped with whipped cream."

Tana washed her hands, hip-bumping Blair a hello. "You should be blogging this, you know? That's a work of art over there."

"If I start blogging about baking, then it might feel like work. And as it is, baking is my outlet." Blair pulled off the purple apron that had been covering a denim skirt and slouchy gray sweater that drooped off one shoulder. "Baking is also my way to bribe my friends into sharing details about their trips with mysterious rich ranchers."

Drying her hands, Tana shook her head. "No need to bribe. I'm going to freely surrender all the dirt because I have no clue what I'm doing, and I need advice."

Blair and Sable exchanged meaningful looks, but Tana didn't bother trying to interpret it. She was too stressed about everything that had happened over the weekend, from her potential return to the poker table, to her very probable heartbreak at the hands of Chase Serrano.

Sable snapped off the volume on the music and slid off the countertop, landing on the tile floor in her tennis shoes. "Right. Everyone, report to the girlfriend war room, aka the dining table. We're going to scarf down sweets and figure this out."

Despite the hurt in her heart and the broken blisters on her heels, Tana couldn't help a small smile at the way her friends marched double time to address her crisis. Her eyes might have stung a little bit, too, because it had been a long time since she had people to look out for her.

Minutes later, they were seated around the antique plank table in the big white wingbacks that served as dining chairs. Bottles of sparkling cider and seltzer rested on a silver platter in the center of the table. Sable filled crystal glasses while Blair served thick slices of the pavlova on stoneware plates.

In as few words as possible, Tana outlined everything. Her grifter past. Her last summer under her father's roof before she went to college. Falling for Chase and the collapse of their relationship thanks to her father's betrayal after she left town. And oh God, what were her friends going to think of her after learning the things she'd done?

"Wait a minute." Blair's fork clattered to her dish as she called a halt to Tana's recap. "Just to clarify, your dad tricked the mother into letting him sell Chase's land while you were already in New York?"

"Right. I had to be in New Paltz in early August that year. My dad married Chase's mother, quietly sold the ranch and then went off the grid a few weeks later." She'd honestly thought everything would be fine in northern Nevada. She'd assumed her father would relocate to Vegas to help her mom with whatever scam she was working there.

So she'd been blindsided to hear what happened. Both her parents had disappeared after Joe Blackstone failed to meet Margot Serrano at the airport for their supposed Paris trip.

Sable lifted her glass to mime a toast toward Blair. "Good point. Chase can only blame Tana so much when she wasn't even in the same state as her dad when he committed the crime."

Blair nodded, picking up her fork again to spear a bite of dessert. "Plus Tana tried to warn Chase to keep an eye on her dad. If she were out of the loop on her father's activities, she couldn't know when or how he planned to strike next." Reaching over to Tana, she squeezed her wrist. "Sorry to interrupt.

You were saying that Chase texted you afterward and that's how you found out what your dad did?"

"Yes. I went to the police and told them everything I knew." It hadn't been much, since he'd quit discussing his plans with her after she said she was leaving for good once she turned eighteen. "Giving them more about my dad's background at least resulted in bigamy charges. Not that he ever faced them in court since he'd already disappeared."

"Does Chase know you cooperated with law enforcement?" Sable narrowed hazel eyes at her across the table.

Tana shrugged, swirling her fork through her dessert. "Hard to say. He had a private investigator find me, so I imagine he knows quite a bit about my past."

"I hope he knows more about your present, which is what matters." Blair bristled as she spoke, her back straightening. "Your choices as an adult have been exemplary. You're not defined by your parents."

The indignation in her voice soothed Tana as much as the words. That her friends believed only good things of her was sweeter than any pavlova.

"Thank you for that. But I'm not sure it will be an exemplary choice to go play poker in the Hamptons, acting as bait for one high roller and one fugitive who happens to be my father." Bad enough she'd be breaking her personal vow never to touch the cards again. She knew that would risk her peace of mind.

But what about the risk to her heart sure to come by engaging in this one last favor for Chase? While he saw her as his ticket to revenge, she couldn't help but see him as much, much more.

Their time together in Nevada had stoked too many old feelings to life again.

Across the table, Sable drummed short pink fingernails against the polished surface, a rhythmic sound like a horse's trot.

When she stopped, she looked back and forth between Tana and Blair. "So take us with you."

Tana stared at her in shock. "I don't follow."

"You're worried about your choices and the stress of this game." Sable met Tana's gaze. "You said it was a party, so why not bring your friends? We can be your on-site sounding board, and we'll have your back."

Blair was already humming affirmative noises while Tana grappled with the idea. Yes, it sounded wonderful to have her friends nearby in a scary situation. But it also sounded awful to have these women—friends she loved and respected—witness the seedy past she yearned to forget.

"I don't know—" she began.

"I do!" Blair protested, banging a palm on the table for emphasis and making her plate jump just a little. "You're not in this alone anymore. You have friends. And friends stick together."

"That's right." Sable nodded slowly. "Who was there for me when I was terrified I lost my baby?" Her hand curled protectively around her belly at just the thought of the scare she'd had early in her pregnancy. It had all been fine, though. Her baby was healthy and developing right on track as she passed the twenty-week mark. "You both were there, making sure I was okay, telling me I could raise this baby even if things didn't work out with Roman." A blissful smile curved her lips. "Which they did."

Blair nodded, winding her ponytail around her fist, and then letting it go again. "And who helped me raise the money for my mother's cancer treatments with the most moving, heartfelt video ever?"

Tana's heart softened at the memory of the footage she'd put together to help fund Amber Westcott's chemotherapy. It had felt good to use her talents behind the camera for such a worthy cause.

"But my situation is so different—"

"We're going," Sable announced, "even if I have to get the party details directly from the hot cowboy."

Blair lifted her glass of sparkling water. "All for one, and one for all, right?"

Sable raised her tumbler and clinked it against Blair's as they both turned expectant gazes her way.

Unused to displays of affection, Tana felt a little awkward at the love. But since she returned it in full measure, she took a deep breath and brought her drink to the center of the table.

"My dad used to say, 'play the hand your dealt like it's the one you wanted.'" She blinked away the emotions threatening to spill from her eyes. "Ladies, thank you for making this hand suck a whole lot less."

They drank to it, sealing the bargain. Tana still wasn't sure how she was going to get through the weekend with Chase when her emotions were so raw. At least her friends had faith in her in spite of her shady past. The confidence boost that gave her made her feel stronger. More ready to face the world she swore she'd left behind forever.

Even if she still had no idea how she was going to resist the man she was falling for all over again.

Three thousand feet in the air, Chase stared down at the gridlock on the Long Island Expressway, grateful for the helicopter service that would take him and Tana directly to Southampton.

"Do you always travel this way when you visit your house in the Hamptons?" she asked from the seat beside him. She smoothed a hand over the shoulder harness of her safety belt, her engagement ring winking in the late-afternoon sun.

She looked different today. She'd rinsed the pink ends from her hair, returning to her natural glossy brown. Her dress and heeled leather boots were both black, but there were no studs in sight. A henna tattoo of a peacock wound around her wrist, the feathers spreading all the way up her forearm. The snake was gone, and so was the stud in her nose. She looked beautiful, but Chase realized he'd grown to enjoy the quirky statements she made with her appearance.

He hoped the lack of spikes in her wardrobe didn't mean she was anxious about the weekend. He already second-guessed himself for asking her to participate in the card game, since it had obviously troubled her. Now that he'd had time to see how much she'd turned her life around after leaving Nevada, he appreciated why she didn't want to be pulled back into that world. And he hated the idea that he was no better than her father, asking her to play another role. But he failed to see how else he could ensure he could lure her father and Warren Carmichael to a card table. Chase had come too far in his quest for revenge to turn around now. The quest had been his objective for eight years.

For now, he refocused on her question as they neared their destination, the chopper humming eastward.

"If I'm going out for a weekend, yes. The traffic is always worse then."

She nibbled her lower lip in a way that made him want to take a bite, too. "I hope my friends make the trip without any trouble tomorrow."

Chase couldn't stop a grin at the memory of her text request for extra party invitations.

"I'm glad you'll have support," he told her honestly, even if a part of him wished she would rely on him for that. Did she think he wouldn't protect her every moment she was under his roof?

He knew that she was only taking part in this weekend for his sake. That alone would have stirred a sense of loyalty even if he hadn't already felt protective of her after what they'd shared at the old homestead on Cloverfield Ranch.

"It might be more than just Sable and Blair who make the trip," she warned him, flicking her thumbnail over the band of the engagement ring as they began their descent. "Some of my castmates expressed interest in coming."

"Really?" He thought back to her performance in the park, surprised she would have mentioned the party to her colleagues. He'd always envisioned Tana as a bit of a loner. "Wasn't today your final show?"

"Yes, it was my farewell to Blanche DuBois." Her smile was tight. Polite. "I got a commercial for next week, but that will only be a day or two of filming. I was thinking about pursuing work on the other side of the camera since I'll have some time on my hands."

Reaching to the floor of the aircraft, she retrieved a satchel-style handbag and pulled a sleek-looking camera from it, brandishing the heavy lens before stuffing the device back in the well-worn bag. The sight of it reminded him that she truly had never profited from her father's scams. She'd worked hard to carve out an honest life for herself since parting from Joe Blackstone's influence.

"While I'm sorry to hear your production ended, I'm glad you've got new options. And of course your castmates are welcome tomorrow night." He tried to shuffle what he knew about Tana to incorporate these new facets.

The filmmaking aspirations. A wealth of friends eager to support her. He'd read about her admission into the brownstone that was a rent-controlled haven for aspiring women artists. She'd impressed some extremely important people with her talent in order to land the spot.

The thought gave him another dose of guilt about what he was asking her to do this weekend.

"Thank you." She opened her mouth to say something else, but just then the helicopter touched down with a jarring motion.

Reflexively, she reached for him, her hand gripping his knee. The denim didn't begin to dull the sensation of her touch. He'd missed it, craved it all week long.

Without taking time to question the wisdom of responding, he covered her fingers with his, trapping her palm against his leg. The chopper came to rest, the blades slowing their rotation while Chase and Tana stared at each other.

Her breaths came quicker, her pupils going dark as her tongue darted along her upper lip. He tracked the movement, his heart thundering in his chest, urging him to act on the heat sparking between them.

"You know why I wanted you to come here with me tonight, the day before the game." It wasn't a question.

He turned her hand over and then cupped it between both of his. In his peripheral vision, he could see the pilot's door opening on the helicopter, but Chase refused to rush this moment with Tana.

"I thought maybe you wanted to go over the layout of the card room. Discuss strategies—"

"No, not at all." His fingers threaded between hers, fitting their hands together. "We can do those things. But I wanted you here tonight to spend time with you. To be with you somewhere nicer than a sleeping bag in a cabin with no central heating."

The quick intake of breath was almost silent, a tiny gasp of surprise or—he hoped—pleasure.

"I liked the cabin," she protested mildly.

The answer pleased the hell out of him, since he'd been content there, too. If anything, it had felt inevitable returning to a place where they'd passed a lot of good hours together long ago.

"You'll like the bed here even more," he promised. "Assuming you want to spend the night in mine."

She shifted in her seat, crossing her legs in a way that made him hope she was feeling the same needy ache that had plagued him all week.

"Why would we do that when—after this game— you'll be returning to your life at Cloverfield and I…" She cast dark eyes toward the roof of the chopper, as if searching for answers anywhere but with him. "I won't be with you?"

He'd known, of course, that this weekend would bring an end to their time together. She'd been extremely accommodating to sign over his lands to him. And now she was helping him entice Warren Carmichael to the card table, and possibly her criminal father, too.

But he had no illusions about a future together. He was deeply attracted, but how could he ever trust her after the way things ended the first time, no matter how much she'd changed? What's more, how would she ever trust him given that he was the one dragging her back into a world she'd worked hard to leave behind? The guilt he'd wrestled all week threatened to ruin all his carefully laid plans. He just needed to focus on seeing this through.

"Isn't that enough reason? If this weekend is all we have, why wouldn't we enjoy it together?" He lifted his free hand to cup her face, tilting it so he could see her better. He stroked his thumb along her cheekbone, imagining having her all to himself for the rest of the night.

For a moment, he thought a shadow of doubt crossed her eyes. But then it was gone, replaced with heat and hunger.

"Okay." Turning her face into his hand, she dragged her teeth along his palm before nipping the base of his thumb. "I'd rather lose myself in the connection we have than waste another second thinking about what tomorrow will bring." Then she reached for her seat belt and clicked the button to unfasten the restraint. "Let's go."

Ten

On the short car ride from the helipad landing to Chase's Southampton home, Tana's body hummed with anticipation. She leaned into the feeling, needing him now more than ever when her fears about tomorrow bubbled so close to the surface.

Chase's touch guaranteed she wouldn't be able to think about anything else but him, and she craved that kind of forgetting. Her heartbeat was a rapid knocking inside her rib cage, every pulse urging her closer as they sat side by side in the back of the chauffeured luxury sedan he'd hired for the trip.

As they drove past a double-gated entrance into a giant horseshoe driveway, however, some of the flushed excitement dissipated. The sleek Mercedes rolled to a stop in front of a palatial gray cedar mansion flanked by complementary buildings that looked like a pool house and guest cottage. Tana felt the full depth of being out of her element. The disparity between her life and Chase's hadn't been quite as apparent on Cloverfield Ranch. But here, in this elegant and lushly landscaped home in one of the world's most exclusive neighborhoods, Tana understood the sort of wealth Chase had amassed in the years they'd been apart.

She hadn't even realized that Chase had exited the vehicle until he pulled open her door himself. He reached a hand in to help her out while the driver removed their bags from the trunk.

For a moment, she hesitated, looking into Chase's gray eyes for a hint of the man she'd fallen for eight years ago. The rancher who'd taught her to ride a horse. The lover who'd claimed her innocence and taught her about pleasure. She needed him now, not the slick billionaire bent on revenge.

"Is everything okay?" he asked, his brow furrowing at whatever he saw reflected in her gaze. His hand dropped to her knee, where he brushed a reassuring touch.

The warmth of his fingers penetrating her knit cotton dress stirred the attraction back to life. Or maybe it was the tenderness in his eyes that suggested he cared how she was feeling. She seized on that, gripping his hand in hers.

Steering it, briefly, higher on her leg. She never broke eye contact, letting him see the way that touch sizzled through her.

His nostrils flared and his chest expanded.

"More than okay," she returned, swiveling on the seat to exit the vehicle. "Just ready to hold you accountable for what you promised me once we arrived."

Chase made quick work of tugging her to her feet, his strong arms banding around her waist. In one motion, he drew her against him so she could feel the hot brand of the erection hidden beneath the gray sport jacket he'd worn with his jeans.

Lowering his mouth to her ear, he spoke softly. "I'm very ready to make good on the promise."

The edge in his voice alone would have made her tremble with need. But the feel of him against her only made it worse, and Tana fought to hold back a hungry whimper.

Chase released her for a quick exchange with the driver, then took her hand to guide her up the wide stone steps and onto a narrow veranda running the length of the gray cedar exterior. After punching in a code on the security system, he opened the front door, then ushered Tana inside a foyer with a sweeping split staircase before admitting the driver carrying their bags.

Between the staircases, Tana could see through the foyer into a library with high coffered ceilings and two fireplaces. There was a formal dining room off to her right and a living area to the left. With white walls and dark wood floors, the house had a minimalist aesthetic that allowed the beautiful architecture to shine.

She swallowed past the swell of nerves, just as she heard the front door close again.

The driver had departed. Leaving them very much alone.

"Hey." Chase stood in front of her again, tilting her chin up, his big body blocking her view of his wealthy world and all the complications that came with it. "Are you still with me?"

She lifted her hands to his chest, smoothing them over the white cotton shirt beneath his jacket, splaying her fingers wide to feel as much of him as possible.

"I am right here with you. Yes," she murmured, gaze dropping to the shirt buttons as she began unfastening the top one.

"Tana." He breathed her name out like a curse or maybe a prayer, stretching the syllables. "What are you doing to me?"

His hands settled around her hips, drawing her to him before his broad palms wandered lower, slowing as they reached the hem of her dress midthigh. There, he fisted the fabric, drawing it tight around her and making her very aware of what he would soon uncover.

Heat thrummed in her belly. Her nipples tightened to hard points.

She licked her dry lips before she could speak. "I hope I'm doing the same thing to you that you're doing to me. You're setting me on fire. Turning me inside out."

"Damn right." He chafed the fabric of her hem

back and forth across her thighs for a moment before letting it go. "Come with me."

Abruptly, he let go of her dress to lead her up one side of the massive staircase. Her legs wobbled a little; she was drunk on her hunger for him and the knowledge that tonight would be the last night they spent together.

After another moment, they were in a luxurious master suite with a private terrace on one side and a skylighted bathroom on the other. While Chase closed the door, she stepped deeper into the room onto the soft gray rug that covered the dark wood floors. The white walls were blank slates save the large windows overlooking the grounds, tall trees all around preventing her from seeing any neighboring houses.

But then her time for gawking was over when Chase's strong forearm curled around her waist to draw her back against him. Air rushed from her lungs at the contact. Her spine arched, hips rocking closer still.

"Did you miss me this week?" she asked before she thought better of it, her voice a breathless wisp of sound.

"You tell me. Does it feel like I missed you?" He lifted her against him, notching his erection between her thighs.

"Yesss," she hissed the final sound between clenched teeth. She squirmed restlessly, needing more of him.

His palm covered her breast, squeezing. Molding.

"Good. Then you'll understand why I can't wait any longer to have you."

Sensation sparked everywhere they touched, sending ripples of pleasure to every nerve ending in her body.

"I can't wait, either." She strained against his grip, but only to turn around so she could see him. "I want to undress you."

He lowered her to the floor, loosening his hold so that she could face him. Before she could go to work on his shirt buttons, however, he lowered his head and covered her lips with his for a drugging kiss.

She forgot everything else, sinking into the feel of his tongue mating with hers. He stroked and explored, conquered and claimed. She clung to him, her fingers fisting around his lapels while he had his way with her mouth.

By the time he let her up for air she was boneless and quivering. Her lashes fluttered, and she slowly raked open her eyes to see Chase stripping off his clothes, his hand at his fly.

She made a mewling sound, half needy, half pleased. His gray eyes flickered to hers, twin silver flames warming her everywhere.

In an instant, she slipped off her leather boots to stand barefoot on the soft carpet, toes curling into the deep pile. As Chase studied her with primal male hunger etched in every feature, Tana reached for the hem of her black knit dress and lifted it up slowly. Slowly.

By the time she shimmed it up and over her head,

Chase was naked and inches from her, his hands landing on her bare ribs to stroke over her body.

"Baby, you're so beautiful," he breathed against her temple, his palms moving to cup her breasts. "I need to see every part of you."

"But I'm ready for you *now*," she confided, smoothing her hands over the hot planes of his hard chest. "You can look while you're inside me."

Restraint slipping fast, Chase had to bite his tongue to keep from laying Tana on the bed and driving deep, over and over. How did this woman get under his skin so fast? Like she belonged there.

Like she'd never left after the first time he'd fallen for her.

He clamped down that thought hard. Because he needed to focus on *her*.

Didn't matter what he was feeling right now. He'd promised her a night to forget everything else but this sizzling connection, and he'd be damned if he didn't deliver.

So as much as he wanted to bury himself in her, he would gladly delay his own gratification to make sure she got off as many times as possible tonight. He wanted to see her reach her peak again and again, and to know that he was the man responsible for taking her there.

"I'm dying to be inside you, too, but I'm going to make it worth your while to wait a little longer, okay?" He snaked an arm around her narrow waist, holding her steady while he dipped the other hand into the satin waistband of tiny black panties. "Trust me?"

She sucked in a gasp as he grazed his fingers over the swollen bud between her legs, but she nodded agreement. He felt the movement where she tucked his head against his chest.

"Good. I think you're already close, don't you?" He teased slow circles around her sex, listening to her breathing quicken, feeling her breasts rise and fall faster. What a privilege to see her this way. To be the one holding her tonight.

His gaze narrowed to her face, watching the flush of color in her cheeks deepen.

Her fingers crept higher on his shoulders as she anchored herself. He quickened his rhythm, knowing her well. Remembering what she needed.

He watched as her lips formed soundless pleas, sensing the tension build as she tilted her hips. And then...

"Oh, Chase." Her body arched hard against him as she ground down into his hand, taking what she wanted. Her throaty cry raked his ears.

The satisfaction of seeing her come apart, feeling her sex pulse and flutter against his hand as he slowed his movements, was almost as good as any release of his own. He wanted to beat his chest with pride at making her come, taking pleasure in knowing he could give that to her. Instead, he kissed her, slow and deep, as he walked her over to the king-size bed in the center of the room.

"I can't wait anymore," she told him as he lifted

her up onto the mattress, laying her gently down in the middle. "No more delaying."

A smile pulled at his lips as he raked her panties down her legs. He got a condom from the nightstand before he covered her with his body.

"Was the last delay so bad?" With one knee, he spread her wider while he unfastened the hooks on her bra with his hand.

"Well, no, actually." Tana slipped her arms around his neck, fingers toying with the hair at the base of his neck in a way that sent shivers down his spine. "I'm not complaining. It's just that—"

He rolled on the condom, his knuckles brushing the slick heat between her thighs as he worked it in place. She'd caught her lip between her teeth at the contact.

"No more delaying," he promised, lifting her arms up over her head.

He meant to pin them there, but as his hand spanned her wrists, the glitter of pink diamonds in her engagement ring caught the light. The satisfaction of seeing the ring there—his ring—was even more potent than what he'd felt over teasing her to release.

The knowledge that she would be giving it back to him tomorrow…

Shutting down the wrongness of that thought, Chase redoubled his focus on her. He edged his way inside her, letting the silky heat of her tight body ease the frustration. With every inch he claimed, the ache of impending loss receded.

When he bottomed out, fully seated inside her, he dropped his forehead to hers.

Bliss.

Utter. Absolute.

He breathed in the citrusy scent of her skin, reveling in how right it felt to be with her this way. When the squeeze in his chest came, a small fissure that threatened to break wide, he knew he needed to move.

Releasing her hands, he started driving his hips into hers. Deeper. Faster. She locked her limber thighs around his waist, meeting every thrust.

The heat built. Raged out of control. Burned over both of them. He would have let it consume them, but he'd promised himself he would make sure she found her peak again before he reached his.

He placed his hands on either side of her shoulders, finding purchase on the bed as he dragged his body over hers slowly, angling himself in a way that provided more friction where she needed it. Sweat popped along his brow as he held himself back, knowing he could get her there, wanting to feel her pulse all around him.

Her fingers scrabbled along his shoulders, nails lightly scoring his spine while her head tossed back and forth. He wanted to bury his face in the silky dark mane of her hair, but he knew she was close.

He nipped her earlobe and then licked it. "No more delays, baby." He threw the words from earlier back at her. "Come for me."

She flew apart so hard, so fast, he didn't have

enough time to watch her. The squeeze of her feminine muscles shattered the last of his restraint, shoving him over the edge into his own release. Waves of pleasure pummeled him, dragging him down and holding him under.

For long moments he let the sensations wash over him, his breath huffing between them like billows. At last, arms damn near weakened from the rush, he lay down beside her and waited until the world righted.

In the quiet aftermath, he felt her snuggle against him, her silky hair blanketing his chest as she found a place for herself there. He managed to flip one side of the duvet over them, enough to cover them as their bodies cooled.

Her left hand lay beside her cheek, the platinum band of her ring a reminder of the pretense he'd forced on her. The fake engagement she hadn't asked for but had undertaken because she felt guilty for her father's actions.

In the stillness of feeling her breathing sync up with his, Chase could admit to himself that had been wrong of him. She had no reason to feel guilty for an act she hadn't committed. A crime she hadn't known her father was planning.

She'd been his scapegoat. A way to avoid placing the blame where it belonged on her father's shoulders. And, yes, on Chase's shoulders too, to a certain extent. He hadn't heeded her warnings about her father, after all. He'd refused to see what was happening all around him that summer, too consumed with falling for Tana to recognize how thoroughly his mother had been ensnared by a con man.

Then, afterward, his bitterness about Tana had blinded him to how Warren took advantage of him, too.

"Don't think about it," Tana said quietly, her words puffing warmly along his chest.

"How do you know what I'm thinking?" He squeezed his eyes closed at the same time his hand cupped her hip. He just couldn't stop wishing he'd thought of some other way to right the wrongs of the past that didn't involve her.

"It's going to be fine." She kissed the place over his heart before settling against him again. "You've never seen me play in a high-stakes game, but I'm good."

Anger at himself bubbled up again. He turned toward her enough to see her, unseating her from the position she'd been in so they faced each other on the bed.

"What if I told you I've changed my mind?" His heart drummed faster at the idea.

"We both know it's too late." Her dark eyes were impossible to read. The light in the room had become dim as the sun lowered in the sky, and there were no lights on in the master suite. "Warren is already flying in for the game, and if my father has heard about the high-stakes poker happening here tomorrow, it's not like we have any way to reach him to tell him it's called off now."

Chase swallowed hard, wondering what the hell

he'd been thinking to choose revenge over…what? He didn't know if he could trust Tana any more now than he ever had.

Just because he'd stopped blaming her for the past didn't mean he'd suddenly be able to trust again. After all, maybe he hadn't just blamed her for her father's crime. Maybe he blamed her for the way things ended between them. For him alone at school in Idaho when he got the news that Joe Blackstone had tricked his mother into marriage in order to rob the family of its land.

It was only natural for Chase to think he'd been tricked into a false relationship, too.

"Maybe it is too late," he admitted finally, the idea dropping on him like a stone. "But we could still host the game without having you play."

"And miss the chance to win back some of the inheritance that Warren stole from you after my father sold off your lands?" She shook her head. "No way. You've worked too hard for this moment to give up on it now."

The vehemence in her words caught him off guard.

He studied her face. "You really want to help me recover it, don't you?"

"I know you might find it tough to believe, but after the life I've lived, Chase, it hurts me more than most people to see someone cheated."

"Even though I've done well for myself in spite of what happened?" Rolling onto his back, he huffed out a sigh. "I noticed your expression when you first saw this house. You're aware that I'm not hurting for the money."

She levered up on her elbow so she could peer down into his face. "Because you worked your tail off to recover what you lost. *No one* deserves to be cheated."

Her dark hair spilled onto his chest while she made her fierce claim. He gathered up some of it and stroked his palm over the length.

"So we won't call off the game." He wanted to kiss her again. To show her how much it meant to him that she was on his side even though it meant going against her own father. Even though it meant opening up her past for others to see. "But I want you to promise me something."

She laid her hands on his chest and then propped her chin in the middle of them. One dark eyebrow arched. "What kind of promise?"

"I know you've gone eight years living your life honestly." He wasn't going to mess that up. Not for anything. "I want you to promise that—even if it looks like you're going to lose to Warren—you won't cheat for my sake. I don't want you to throw away your long streak of living honestly for me."

Her full lips drew together in a frown. Even in the dim light, he could have sworn a chill came into her eyes.

"You still don't trust me?"

"It's not about trust. It's about how hard you've worked to build a different life." He was proud of her for that. "You've achieved so much."

Her gaze narrowed. "It hasn't been hard work not to cheat people. It actually comes very easily to me to be honest."

"Of course I know that now. And I don't want you to think that I'm asking you to do anything different than you've done for eight years." He didn't understand why he'd offended her, but he could feel her pulling back even as they lay there together. "Either you win at cards or you don't, but there's no need to stack the odds in your favor."

Tana dragged a throw blanket from the far end of the bed and wrapped it around herself as she moved to sit on the edge of the mattress. It wasn't lost on him that she was pulling away, closing herself off.

"Fine. I promise not to cheat." She slid off the bed and moved in the direction of the bathroom, tossing her hair over her shoulder. "For now, we should eat. All the sex made me ravenous."

She closed the bathroom door behind her before he could respond. Something was off in her response. Was she offended that he'd asked her not to employ the old tricks of her days in a con artist family?

Maybe it would have made her play easier. Less stressful.

Then again, he understood she hadn't wanted to play in the first place. Perhaps she was frustrated that he wanted to dictate how she approached a game she hadn't wanted to be in to start with.

Rising from the bed, he tried not to dwell on it. His plans were in place. She'd told him not to cancel. And he still had a whole night in front of him with Tana before he confronted the men who'd wronged him.

Or at least one of them, if her father didn't show up.

Chase would use every minute of the time they had left to show her he believed in her, to make up for the hurt he'd caused. He just hoped that would be enough to help them through whatever tomorrow brought.

Eleven

Staring into the dressing room mirror the next afternoon, Tana leaned on the marble countertop of the elegant vanity table to slick on her eyeliner, flicking the end to create a cat's eye. Her stomach was full of butterflies. With so much riding on tonight, it took all her theater training in tackling nerves to keep her hand from shaking.

She'd spent far more time on her appearance today than normal, knowing that—like Yogi Berra had famously said of baseball—poker was 90 percent mental. That meant she needed time to get her head focused before the other players began arriving. That seemed easiest to do while locked in the master suite dressing area, far from Chase and all the confusing feelings that last night had unearthed.

Remembering their time together threatened to tumble all the precarious barriers she'd erected around her heart. It had been more than just phenomenal sex. There'd been a synchronicity, an anticipation of each other's needs. And afterward, there'd been the long hours of holding each other. Sharing the happy memories of their past instead of only the bad ones, both of them determined to savor the moment for however long they could.

Switching to the other eye and running the black makeup over her lash line, Tana just wished that they'd never had the conversation about cheating at cards. A conversation in which he'd asked her not to cheat, which felt to her like an implication that she might have otherwise. It had hurt. Especially after the night they'd shared.

Flinching slightly at the memory, she messed up the cat's eye, smudging the line at the end close to her temple.

"Damn it." She set down the brush and searched her makeup bag for remover to clean up the mistake.

Hadn't she told herself not to think about Chase? About his lack of trust in her? Her stomach knotted. She knew tonight would be the end of things between them. He'd take back his ring after she helped him win the money Warren had swindled from him. She would return the land her father had won from Warren. Balance would be restored in Cloverfield. Then, she and Chase would go their separate ways for good, and she'd tell herself that it was okay since he still didn't trust her anyway.

Even though she was doing all of this for him.

So maybe it wasn't just her stomach that was in knots. Her heart felt like it was being yanked in two different directions, too.

Rubbing a cotton swab dotted with makeup remover over the black blotch, Tana heard a knock on the bedroom door. Nerves stretched thin, she didn't move from the dressing table. She didn't trust her knees to hold up.

"Chase, I told you. I need to focus." In theory, she was giving herself a pep talk about playing poker again. Remembering all the old wisdom her dad had taught her from an early age.

A pair of balls beats every other hand, sweetheart. Remember the power of bluffing.

Or, *play the man, not the hand.*

She could spout the maxims for hours. If only she could concentrate on them and not Chase.

"It's not the hot cowboy, girlfriend. Let us in!" a distinctly feminine voice called through the door.

Relief flooded through her at the sound of Sable's thick Southern drawl. Tossing aside the makeup tools, Tana rushed to the door and unbolted it. As she swung open the barrier, her friends swarmed in. Blair carried her professional cosmetics kit that looked like a heavy silver tackle box. Sable had black garment bags with Zayn Designs printed on the side in gold lettering.

Tana glanced into the hallway behind them, but the landing was empty. She could hear the catering staff downstairs in the kitchen, however. No doubt

Chase's work crews had arrived to transform the great room into a card room, while the caterers would be arranging the hors d'oeuvres and drinks appropriate for an exclusive party of high rollers.

Locking the door behind them, she turned to see Blair settling the makeup kit on the vanity and Sable hanging the garment bags in the huge closet that opened off the bathroom. They were dressed casually in jeans and T-shirts, but Tana guessed their gowns for later were contained in the garment bags.

Blair, who wore a pink blazer over her white T-shirt, turned to hug her. "The cavalry is here, hon. I can finish your makeup for you."

Tana squeezed her friend back, breathing in the rose and vanilla scent of her long blond hair, which fell in loose curls to her shoulders. Tana might not be used to hugging, but she needed the love today. Desperately.

"Thank you. I was turning my cat's eye into a black eye." She let go of her friend, so grateful for the distraction.

And the friendship.

Blair bent her knees to see Tana's face better, angling her own underneath. "I can turn it into a smoky eye. It'll be gorgeous."

Before Blair had finished the assessment, Sable was by Tana's side, sliding an arm around her waist.

"And wait until you see what you're wearing. You're going to die." Her drawl drew out the last word into an extra syllable as she tipped her dark head onto Tana's shoulder. "I needed to dress you two extra sexy tonight since this baby bump is forcing me into muumuus and caftans."

"Oh, please," Tana retorted as Blair drew her back into the chair at the vanity table. "You were buying maternity clothes ten seconds after that pregnancy test and you know it."

"Okay. Guilty." Sable smiled as she moved to unzip one of the garment bags. "It's more fun to think about pregnancy outfits when you still have a waist." She wrenched off the bag with a flourish. "But what do you think of this?"

The red silk gown she'd revealed was breathtaking. The halter neck had plunging décolletage and a floor-length hem. The lines were clean and simple, uninterrupted by flounce or ribbon so the attention would be on the feminine form beneath the fabric. And before Tana could wonder what the back looked like, Sable spun the hanger to show off the way the dress would appear backless once it was on, the fabric ending just below the waist.

Speechless, Tana could only stare from one amazing friend to the other.

Sable didn't appear to need words, however. She winked at Tana.

"I know, right? You thought the gowns I sent you for that wedding were too much of a fairy princess vibe. So this time I went with more of a queen of diamonds look." Then, pulling out a shoebox from the bottom of the open garment bag, she tugged off the top. "Even the shoes are hot-to-trot red."

Overcome by the gestures, Tana felt herself relax

the tiniest bit for the first time all day. Yes, tonight was going to be difficult. Scary.

But she'd have a new kind of armor to wear as she entered the card room.

Better yet, she'd have her friends at her side.

Exhaling a deep breath, Tana let Blair tip her chin up into the light she'd repositioned in order to work on Tana's face.

"Okay, I'd better get busy," she murmured half to herself, sweeping Tana's hair into a clip to keep it out of the way. Then, opening her makeup kit to lift the accordion-style trays inside, Blair continued, "When we first were at the door, you said you had to focus. You mean on the game?"

Behind them, Sable kicked off her shoes and paired her phone with a speaker near the bed, filling the room with guitar-heavy rock music. It was the kind of thing they'd always played on their Friday nights together in the brownstone. And even that small nod to their friendship helped Tana relax a little more.

She would enjoy this time with her friends because their days together in the Brooklyn apartment were numbered. Sable spent fewer and fewer evenings with them as her job and fiancé vied for her time. Plus, she needed to prepare for her baby. Blair was planning a future with Lucas Deschamps, heir to a cosmetics empire and her former boss.

As for Tana, she wouldn't be able to afford even the rent-controlled apartment much longer if another acting gig didn't come through. Who knew how many more moments she'd have like this with her friends? Because while she'd treasure them for life, the days as roommates were special.

"Yes. I've been trying to remember everything I know about poker so I can psych myself up to play." She watched Blair choose an eyeshadow palette and a brush.

"Would it help you to have quiet to think? Or did you want to talk through strategy out loud?" Blair swirled the narrow brush in a metallic gray powder.

Tana closed her eyes in preparation for the makeup, grateful for the friend time. Soaking it up like healing medicine for her nerves.

"I'd love to talk it out." She felt safe here, in the company of these ladies who trusted her. Who didn't feel the need to warn her not to cheat. "For starters, I've just been thinking through all the things my dad used to say. Not that it was such great wisdom, but it helps take me back to a time when I played every night. When it felt easy."

Blair hummed, half to the beat of the song and half in response to Tana. "Like what? Know when to hold 'em? And know when to fold 'em?"

Tana laughed, a little more unease floating away. "Sort of. For one thing, he used to say, 'Tana, if you're staring at your cards, you're not watching the other players look at theirs. Read the game. Read the players.'"

And for the next hour, she dug deep to remember all the things she'd buried eight years ago. About her father. About poker. About the games they'd played together back when he'd had fun showing off his card-playing protégé. Surprisingly, it wasn't all bad. There'd been some good memories in the awful ones. A few nights where they'd pulled Robin Hood–style wins at the table, beating rich whales who treated the cocktail waitresses like crap. Then Tana and her dad had tipped those waitresses with almost all the winnings, walking out of the card room with little more money in their pockets than what would buy them a big breakfast.

She talked and reminisced, remembering the old game rhythms, not realizing how much time was passing. Until, suddenly, she was standing in front of a full-length mirror letting Sable zip her into the sexiest dress Tana had ever worn in her life.

The red silk caressed without clinging, following the lines of her body like it had been made for her. Blair fastened the halter neck tighter, making sure Tana wouldn't fall out of it. But there was no room for underthings.

Still, the dress was a layer of confidence. For years she'd worn spikes and an abundance of eye makeup, daring the world to judge her for her past. But this was a different kind of costume. A look that said she was a woman comfortable in her own skin. Between the red silk on her body and the exquisite makeup on her face that made her look…well, *queenly*, Tana felt like a new woman.

Bold. Ready.

She would not resort to any card tricks tonight. But she absolutely had to win. Only then would she be able to walk away from Chase with her head held high, knowing she'd done everything in her power to right her father's wrongs.

Tana might not be able to save her heart from breaking. But she would heal an old wound and—just maybe—forgive herself in the process.

Chase roamed the Hamptons house shortly before game time, double-checking his preparations as guests began arriving for the cocktail hour. There were plenty of locals and a few business associates who weren't there for poker, preferring to mingle and—in some cases—preview the house that Chase had renovated and would be putting on the market soon.

Those guests were in the conservatory overlooking the grounds. The night was warm enough that there was an outdoor bar set up near the pool house.

But Chase was more interested in the living area that had been set up as a card room.

Spotting the professional dealer he'd brought in for the evening, he paused to ask, "Do you have everything you need?"

"Yes, sir. Thank you," the silver-haired gentleman replied, glancing up from his open box of cards and chips. He wore a bow tie and vest over his shirtsleeves, and a gold signet ring flashing on his pinkie as he shuffled cards on the black cloth playing surface in the middle of the antique mahogany table. "I'll be ready at game time."

Chase nodded his thanks, looking over the ten

leather-upholstered chairs—enough for the dealer, seven confirmed players, and two empty seats to accommodate possible guests who'd failed to RSVP.

Joe Blackstone, for instance, could still show.

Or, for all Chase knew, Tana's missing father could be using an alias and had already confirmed a spot. The man had certainly employed fake identities in the past. Still, Chase had checked the backgrounds of the confirmed players and felt confident none of them was Joe.

He'd wanted to show the list to Tana, but she'd retreated from him completely today. He shouldn't have extracted the promise about not cheating. He understood why that unsettled her. Had he really needed it? He'd told himself that he was beyond the mistrust. Especially since their night together had been unforgettable, every moment of it seared into his memory forever. But this morning, she'd insisted she needed quiet to mentally prepare for the game, the coolness suggesting she hadn't forgotten about his lack of faith in her. She'd locked the door to the master suite, only admitting her girlfriends who'd arrived that afternoon.

So he'd been forced to wrestle all over again with the idea that he should call off this game. Haul her back to his bed and tell her she didn't need to recover what he'd lost eight years ago. He didn't blame her, so he couldn't possibly ask her to do any more to help him recover the last of his inheritance.

It was money that had ceased to matter, other than in principle. So why was he still moving forward?

Why undermine the small amount of trust he thought they'd rebuilt? Unless his confidence in her wasn't as solid as he thought.

"Damn it." He pounded his fist on the bar, making a huge arrangement of purple irises jump in their sleek white vase.

"Pregame jitters?" a seductive feminine voice asked from behind him.

Whirling around, he faced the woman he'd been missing all day. A stunning vision in red tonight, Tana rivaled any Hollywood star in beauty and elegance. Soft waves framed her face, a jeweled clip on one side winking in the light of the chandelier. A hint of glitter just under her brow bone and red lipstick were fanciful touches, along with the diamond drop earrings swinging against her dark hair.

But the dress she wore…no, it was her gorgeous body inside the dramatic dress that would have every jaw dropping tonight. The red silk halter plunged deep between her breasts, showing a hint of the high, subtle curve of each. Skinny straps tied the thin fabric around her neck, making it look like a good breeze might blow the whole thing off her.

"No one at that table will have their mind on poker tonight. Not while you're wearing that dress," he growled quietly as he pulled her to him, needing to feel her. Reassure himself that he still had the right to touch her.

But for how much longer? a contrary part of his brain wanted to know.

"That would be an amazing advantage, but I'm

not sure I'll be able to distract anyone else as thoroughly as I seem to have distracted you." She edged back a step, peering up into his face. "Is everything all right? You sounded upset a moment ago."

Now that he'd recovered—mostly—from the sight of her in that dress, Chase noticed the tension in her bare shoulders. The hint of anxiety in her dark eyes.

"I'm fine. Just still wondering if this is a mistake." He took her hand now that he was no longer touching the rest of her. His fingers skimmed over the ring on her finger, wishing things were different between them. That they'd met under different circumstances. "I don't want to subject you to something that's going to cause you more stress."

"At this point, I'm counting on a win to be healing for me. For both of us. You'll see that I'm not a cheat." She withdrew her fingers from his. Straightening the jewelry, she pivoted to look out over the card room. Away from him. "Besides, we're so close to achieving everything you wanted when you first approached me at the play. I'm not giving up before we close the deal."

Her cool words felt like they'd come from a stranger, even though she was giving him what he'd wanted. And, as gorgeous as she was beside him right now, he missed the way she sparred with him. The tattoos and spikes. The pink in her hair.

He'd turned her into this remote beauty tonight by asking her to play a role she'd never wanted.

"Tana—"

"There's Warren." She pointed to the rancher entering the card room, his slick blue suit paired with elaborately stitched leather cowboy boots. "And I think I see a few faces from my play behind him. I should say hello."

Damn it.

Chase nodded stiffly, knowing he couldn't escape Warren Carmichael if he wanted to as the man charged toward him across the great room.

"We'll talk later," Chase reminded her. "You've avoided me all day, but I need to speak with you after the game."

He wasn't ready to let her go tonight. He didn't know what that meant, or how they could spend more time together. But after the night they'd shared, he hungered to explore the option.

"Of course." Her smile showed no teeth. With a brief nod, she seemed to float through the growing crowd toward her arriving friends.

And Chase knew he'd just seen her poker face. It boded well for the game table, since he didn't have a chance in hell of reading her and he'd doubt anyone else would be able to, either.

But as for what it meant for them? He wondered if she'd already retreated so far from him there'd be no winning her back.

Her father wasn't coming.

Tana's thoughts turned more and more to that realization as the evening wore on. She'd lost track of how many hands had been played so far, but she'd started off the evening in the button seat—an advantageous position since she was able to place her bet last—and she'd won a significant hand the second time she held that position.

By now, the table had shrunk to four players, and she had a good feel for her opponents. Warren's play had not impressed her, but she knew better than to underestimate him. So far, she'd played with the cash that Chase had staked for the game, but she knew the time would come when she'd need to put the deed to Warren's former lands on the table.

He'd raised frequently, sometimes unwisely, no doubt in an effort to make her put the paperwork in the pot. But she wouldn't be goaded into playing that game. She wanted to recoup Chase's lost cash inheritance every bit as much as Warren longed for the return of the property he'd lost to her father long ago.

And where was Chase?

She risked a quick glance up from the table, missing his presence in the room. He'd sat at the bar across from her for the first hour or so, visiting with her girlfriends until Sable and Blair had disappeared out onto the patio. But Chase had lingered at least a few hands afterward, though the spot was vacant now. Even more telling, she didn't *feel* him nearby. How funny was it that, just days after seeing him again, she could already sense him when he was close?

Her chest ached at the thought of breaking that connection for good. Far more than the other, surprise ache of not seeing her dad tonight. She'd put him out of her mind for years, knowing he was a bad influence. A criminal. But a therapist at her college had once told her that it wasn't a crime to have love in her heart even for people who hurt her. She could feel those emotions without letting them hurt her again.

And yeah, in spite of everything, there'd been a piece of her that had wanted to see him again. Or rather, there was a piece of her that hoped her father would want to see *her*. Which, clearly, he did not.

Now, folding a weak hand, Tana bided her time until the dealer called for a short break in the action. Once the hand finished, the pot going to the quiet older woman named Odina at the far end of the table, Tana stood to stretch her legs. The real work would begin in the second half of the evening when play was elevated.

All the remaining players had taken one another's measures. Odina, the stoic older lady, played a conservative but effective game. Warren, the hothead rancher, played with more reserve than Tana had anticipated, but he still made aggressive plays that could bite him in the end. Then there was Tana and a jovial Eastern European man named Cyrilo who spoke with such a thick accent that Tana had briefly wondered if it could be her dad in disguise— changing his voice along with his appearance.

But that thought had been fleeting, given he was at least three inches taller than her father, a symptom of how much she'd secretly hoped her dad might make an appearance after all this time.

Frankly, it ticked her off that she'd given him so much thought when he didn't care if he ever atoned for his crimes. Or atoned for being a sorry excuse for a father.

Tana picked up speed as she neared the doors out to the patio where she hoped to find Blair and Sable, or some of her friends from the *Streetcar* performance. The security guard, Lorraine, had brought Megan, the actress who'd played Stella. They were dating now, and it had been so kind of them to support her. She wanted to see them before the inevitable heartbreak that awaited her at the end of the evening when Chase took back his ring.

"Tana?" The unfamiliar voice behind her stopped her just short of the open French doors.

Turning, she saw Odina a few steps behind her. The older woman had her head down as she seemed to be digging in her oversize handbag. With her neutral-colored pantsuit and dark, blunt haircut, Odina was the kind of player who would have been easy to underestimate. The clothes were a great misdirection now that she thought about it. Smarter than Tana's fiery red dress actually, even though she wouldn't trade Sable's generous fashion help for anything.

"Did you lose something?" Tana asked, taking a step back into the corridor that she thought led to a guest bathroom and maybe a home gym.

"Just looking for my denture glue. I'm so embarrassed." The woman peered up from her handbag, holding a set of false teeth in her hand.

Something about the woman's face seemed off. Or

familiar somehow. But she didn't want to stare when Odina had just said she was embarrassed.

"Erm. You think it's in your bag?" she suggested helpfully, trying to pull her gaze away from how the lack of the false teeth changed the shape of the woman's mouth.

Even her cheeks looked different…

"Took you long enough to recognize me," Odina said, her voice utterly altered. Masculine. And yes, very familiar now.

Her father.

Much thinner. With different colored hair and eyes, and maybe some cheek plumpers in his mouth.

But what had thrown her the most was that she'd never thought to look for him in a feminine disguise.

"Oh my God." Tana covered her mouth to prevent an outburst, not quite sure what her next move should be.

Scream? Call Chase?

Or take this break in the game to ask her dad where the hell he'd been for eight years?

"Come on." Her father took her wrist in a grip that was far from feeble and pulled her down the hall. "We need to talk before the next hand."

Twelve

Chase had searched for Tana during the break, but didn't find her. Then, before the game resumed, Warren Carmichael had dragged him into a conversation. So Chase was only able to watch as the players reconvened around the table, the group whittled down to just four competitors and the dealer.

An hour into the next tense round of poker play, a glass appeared in Chase's vision.

"You look like you could use a drink." The speaker, Roman Zayn, held his own beverage in his other hand. Beside him stood Lucas Deschamps.

Chase had met the two men briefly when they arrived a couple of hours ago. They were the respective partners of Tana's friends Sable and Blair. Chase knew them both by reputation since his own investments required a relentless eye on the business world. Fashion and cosmetics weren't areas of particular familiarity for Chase, coming from ranching. But as the personal luxury goods market was worth almost $300 billion worldwide, he certainly knew their companies.

"Is it that obvious?" Chase asked quietly, in deference to the ongoing game. He accepted the glass, recognizing the pecan and caramel scents of a top-shelf bourbon. He took a sip appreciatively, confirming his guess.

The drink provided a pleasant burn but didn't come close to easing the tension that had settled thick in the card room nearby. The bar was far enough from the action that they could speak here, although in general, the conversation grew more muted in the great room as the stakes rose at the poker table. The party outside remained in full swing, however, the music and laughter from the pool deck area still audible over the sounds of the bartender mixing drinks and the dealer narrating the game.

Roman, the owner of a fashion label and the soon-to-be father of Sable Cordero's baby, was built like a soccer fullback, all shoulder and muscle. With dark hair and eyes, he slouched into the corner seat at the bar. "More than obvious. You looked ready to grind your molars to dust."

Lucas Deschamps dropped into the seat on Chase's other side, his height and lean form all casual grace. He looked like he'd been to plenty of parties in the Hamptons in his time, his tailored navy jacket and relaxed air in keeping with his wealthy East Coast upbringing. "I've never understood this game. Care to interpret what's happening over there? Tana looks like she's holding her own."

Tana's name on another man's lips snagged Chase's attention sharply away from the woman and toward the speaker.

"You know her, then? I mean, aside from just a nodding acquaintance as Blair's roommate?" Chase took another sip of the bourbon, feeling it safe to look away from the game since Tana wasn't betting. The older woman, Odina, looked like she was going all in on this hand, though.

The pot was already hefty.

"I'll say." Lucas's smile was wry as he plucked a cherry from the bartender's stash and tossed it in his mouth. "She was Blair's personal security team while I was trying to court her. At the end, I was lucky to get past Tana to see Blair after I screwed up and fired her."

Chase lifted an eyebrow at Lucas while the next player—the Eastern European guy with a thick accent—deliberated his bet. "You fired your girlfriend?"

"Well, no. But that's how Tana saw it, and she didn't let me forget it." Lucas stretched long legs in front of him, Italian loafers toeing the carpet. "She made me bring my A game to winning back Blair, that's for sure."

Chase smiled with satisfaction to hear it. "She's

not someone to mess with," he agreed, his chest swelling with pride.

On his other side, Roman leaned closer to confide, "Tana convinced Sable that they could raise my child in the brownstone—without me—and told her to take her time deciding if I was the right choice for her."

While Chase wanted to inform him that it sounded like wise advice to any expectant mother, the shadow of fear that lurked in the back of the big guy's eyes told Chase how much the idea of being separated from his child had shaken him.

"I'm glad it worked out for you," he told the other man sincerely, his admiration for Tana growing still more. "Congratulations to you and Sable."

"Thank you." Roman managed to touch his glass to Chase's almost soundlessly before he glanced up at the poker table. "Hey, what did Tana just add to the pot?"

Jerking his attention back to the game, Chase saw a piece of paper on top of the pile of chips.

She'd bet the deed to the lands Warren wanted.

Chase's gaze went to Warren Carmichael, recognizing the greed in the other man's eyes at the same time the dealer nodded, seeming to accept Tana's bet. "Player three raises with property assigned a cash value of fifty thousand."

The lands were worth more than that. Especially to Warren, who used the acreage to move his cattle from one section of his ranch to another. But they'd wanted Warren to take this bet when Tana made it.

Had she chosen the right hand to dangle the carrot?

Heart in his throat while he waited to see if his old enemy would take the bait, Chase's gaze slid around to the others at the table. Cyrilo, the Eastern European high roller, had folded. Odina, the older woman, had gone all in.

And as Chase's eye was about to skim past the petite woman's black bob, he noticed the way the lady glanced up at Tana.

A quick, furtive moment of eye contact.

Or had she winked?

His instincts twitched uneasily, spine tingling with new awareness. What was he missing here? Chase glanced around the room, confident someone else must have seen the exchange if it had actually happened. There were plenty of observers.

Yet who else here knew Tana's history besides him?

Chase could hardly pay attention to Warren's next move, though he knew his nemesis was over a barrel. He'd either have to fold and lose everything he'd put into the pot already, or match Tana's bet to stay in the hand.

And even though this was the moment Chase had been waiting for—a revenge scenario he'd long dreamed about—he realized in the moment it didn't matter at all. Hell, he'd rather have lost all the money and the land, too, if it meant he'd never put Tana in a scenario where she could have been tempted to—

No.

His heart pounded harder. She'd promised him she wouldn't cheat, and he trusted her. She wasn't the same woman he'd known eight years ago, and he'd witnessed firsthand how hard she'd worked to turn her life around. Besides, she didn't know the older woman who'd winked at her.

Did she?

Chase must have missed something—Warren going all in—while Chase's old demons whispered in his ear. Because a moment later, the dealer was announcing the winner of the hand—Tana—while the room erupted into applause.

"That was amazing," Lucas acknowledged on his left side. "She had a royal flush the whole time."

On Chase's other side, Roman gave a wolf whistle before clapping Chase on the shoulder. "Nicely done. Congrats, man. Your girl is a poker champion."

Trying to shake off the uneasy feeling, Chase's attention fixed on Tana again. She was acknowledging congratulations from Cyrilo while Warren walked away from the table in disgust. Still, Tana's dark eyes sought Chase's as the dealer called for another break.

Why didn't Tana look happier? She'd just won the biggest pot of the night, worth over a million thanks to the no-limit stakes. Enough to refund the cash inheritance Warren had taken from him.

Yet Chase saw only worry etched on her pretty features.

"Excuse me," he muttered to his companions, charging toward her to find out what was wrong.

Shouldn't she be pleased? Or maybe she simply

hadn't wanted the evening to end either, since they'd planned to go separate ways after tonight.

Of course, he'd hoped to renegotiate. He just needed to tell her about the feelings stirring inside him.

"Congratulations, Tana." He greeted her with a kiss on the cheek, appreciating the comfort that came with wrapping an arm around her narrow waist.

But then he realized she was shaking like a leaf.

"Chase." Her voice was low and urgent in his ear. "We have to go outside. Follow Odina."

Rearing back, he tried to compute what she'd just said. Tried to figure out why she was trembling.

"Odina?" Had the other woman cheated somehow? Maybe that was what the wink had been about. "What about her?"

His attention was already spanning the room, searching for the older lady.

"It's my father," Tana confided in the softest of whispers, jabbing a pin into all of Chase's overinflated hopes about her. "In disguise."

Just that fast, she'd gutted him.

Chase hadn't been wrong about the look exchanged between Tana and her ex-con parent. She'd cheated her way to the bitterest of victories.

Tana felt Chase stiffen beside her, but he followed her out to the pool patio where she'd seen her father retreat.

Her dad was sick—dying of pancreatic cancer—and probably shouldn't have been out at all. He'd lost a tremendous amount of weight, but he'd promised her he just wanted to sit in on the hand to see his daughter compete one last time at the game he'd taught her.

What was she supposed to say?

Still, she knew Chase would be angry. But she also trusted that he would understand when her father turned himself in as he'd promised to once the other guests left for the evening. Her father didn't want to taint her evening or the victory that—even two hours ago in their private reunion—her dad knew she would have. He'd had total faith in her ability to pull it off fairly.

Now, Joe waited for them out on the beach, the waves of the Atlantic audible as Tana skirted the pool house that marked the edge of Chase's party.

"Where are we going?" Chase hooked an arm in her elbow, hauling her to a stop just before her feet hit the sand.

They stood on the flagstone path that wound between the tennis courts and the beach. The late-summer wind blew stronger here, with fewer trees to block it. She gripped the skirt of her silk dress to keep it from flying up.

"My dad's out on the beach, waiting for the party to end." She had so much to tell him. Her brain had been so fixated on the game and winning back what Warren Carmichael had stolen from Chase that she hadn't really let herself process the news that her father was back. That he was terminally ill. "He's turning himself in, Chase."

"And you *believe* him?" The sharp edge in his voice cut straight through all the tender and raw emotions of the night. The whole day.

The last week and a half.

Gripping the gown tighter, she willed herself to stay strong against those feelings for fear they'd knock her right down.

"Yes. I do. He had no other reason to come here tonight, other than to see me one last time—"

Chase's bark of cynical laughter cut her off and sliced through her. "He hid out for eight years, never contacting you. Never showing his face. But suddenly he wants to see you on the night when there's a no-limits game he thinks he has a shot of winning?" He shook his head. "Excuse me if I'm skeptical."

His disbelief hurt, but she understood. Steeling herself, she hoped Chase could still separate his feelings for her criminal father versus his feelings for her. After all, the time she'd spent with Chase over the last ten days must have meant something to him.

He might not love her, the way she now realized she'd never stopped loving him. But he must care for her.

"I know you have every reason to doubt him, but I hope you won't doubt me." She wanted him to know why her dad had left the Nevada lands in trust for her. What he'd hidden there. She'd learned a lot in her conversation with her father. But first she needed Chase to listen.

The muscle in his jaw worked back and forth as he seemed to consider this, the Atlantic wind tousling his hair, brushing strands in his eyes. The fissure in her chest split open wider at how long it took him to speak again.

"I wish I didn't have reason to doubt you," he said finally, his gray eyes dark. Flat.

She couldn't blame it on the night sky, either. There was a full moon that lit his expression well.

"W-what do you mean?" Her voice wobbled. No amount of spikes and studs, tattoos and piercings would have been enough to ward off the pain his hard voice was inflicting.

"I mean, I saw the look you and your father exchanged across the poker table right before that last bet. It seemed off when I thought it was an old woman winking at you. But now that I know it was your father…" He shook his head, his expression grave as he seemed to size her up and find her wanting. "I thought you weren't going to resort to the old tactics. Collusion is still cheating."

The thin ice she'd been skating on with him all week broke right under her feet. A new, frigid chill surrounded her, dragging her under. Tana welcomed that cold, praying it would keep her numb enough to walk away from Chase Serrano before he saw how he'd just devastated her.

She'd need her guardian angel, though, to pull it off. She kept the thought of those protective wings in mind as she reached for the engagement ring on her finger and took it off.

"How. Dare. You." She articulated the words carefully between shivers so he wouldn't hear her devastation. She was proud of how she'd managed it. Reaching for Chase's hand, she slammed the jewelry into his palm and closed his fingers around it. "Take this. Take your land. Take your winnings. I never want to see you again."

"Tana, wait." Chase might have reached for her. She thought she felt his fingers brush her shoulder.

But she was keeping the numbness around her like a protective shawl, her sole focus on finding her father so she could say goodbye. She'd have to tell Chase the rest of the news in a letter. Registered mail, so he couldn't ignore it.

Because one thing was certain. She would not be speaking to him again. She didn't want him to see the love he'd just crushed to pieces under his boot.

Thirteen

Chase didn't know how much time had passed when he opened the fist containing the engagement ring. He stood rooted to the spot where Tana had left him, her words circling around his head, berating him.

Telling him over and over again how badly he'd misjudged her.

What had he just done?

The Atlantic wind blew harder, stirring grains of sand off the beach to pelt his face. The moment he'd uttered the word *collusion* he'd witnessed the blood drain from Tana's lovely face. In the moonlight, that had meant she'd turned three shades paler. Even her lips had gone slack with shock.

Immediately, he'd realized he'd blown it. He'd let his fears get the best of him. Instead of hearing her out, he'd taken the offensive, scared of being fooled again.

Tana had been facing down her own fears for his sake, sitting at that poker table tonight even though she hadn't wanted to ever play again. But he'd been so hell-bent on a revenge that it hadn't mattered he'd put her in that position anyway.

Then, when she'd needed him to conquer his own fears, what had he done? He'd lashed out like a coward, believing the worst.

Loss hollowed out his insides.

The sounds of the party—dance music and laughter—reminded him he had a responsibility to his guests back at the house. But he couldn't bring himself to care. Instead, his gaze went out to the beach. In the moonlight he could see the figure of Tana. Beside her, the outline of another person.

Her father?

He noticed Tana had just walked away from the other figure, and the rest of the beach was empty. Tana moved farther away from the party, heading in the direction of a public parking lot for beach access. Chase longed to intercept her, hating the idea of her wandering around Southampton after midnight.

But he knew she'd meant it when she told him she never wanted to see him again. He might not be able to change her mind about that, but if he hoped to have any chance of an audience with her again, he guessed tonight was not the time to press the issue.

Stuffing down his fear at that possibility, he directed his footsteps toward the other person on the beach instead.

Sand slid into his dress shoes, but he ignored the grit to focus on the man dressed in a woman's pantsuit. This was Joe Blackstone? While he'd never been a big man, the guy had lost at least fifty pounds. But as Chase closed the distance, he could see the figure had ditched the black wig to reveal thin gray wisps of hair blowing to one side. He'd taken off his shoes, his pants rolled up just below the knee as he checked a phone screen.

"Joe?" Chase asked as he neared, the wind apparently masking the sound of his approach.

The light on the phone screen went off and Tana's father pivoted toward him.

"Chase." The older man gave a nod of acknowledgment, his face expressionless. "I was just checking on the status of my ride. The local cops agreed to pick me up when I told them I'm wanted in Nevada."

In the moonlight, Chase could see he must have removed some of his makeup from his Odina disguise. His cheekbones had fallen, too, as if they'd been plumped by some artificial means. Even the teeth were different.

"You're really turning yourself in?" Chase couldn't believe that of Joe Blackstone, not even once Chase realized that—of course—Tana had not cheated. "I assumed you just told that to Tana."

The con man shook his head. "I'm done lying to her. To everyone. Five years of Gamblers Anonymous has taught me better habits."

"Yet you gambled tonight," Chase couldn't help but point out, still not sure he believed anything from the man who'd duped his mother. Broken her heart.

"I told Tana why. I knew this game was your way of luring me out of hiding, and it was high time I paid the price for what I did to you and your mom. I don't mind serving the time for that now, but I couldn't resist the chance to see my girl play at the top of her game tonight." Joe flashed a hint of white teeth in a smile.

She shouldn't have been playing at all, Chase thought to himself, hating that he'd asked her to. Hating that he hadn't just enjoyed the gift of being with her while he'd had the chance.

Joe tipped his face into the wind, folding his arms across his chest. "She was magnificent. I know I shouldn't be so proud that I gave her a skill some consider a vice. But she could compete at the highest levels. Make a fortune in tournament play if she chose."

Seeing the expression on the other man's face put the wink he'd seen at the poker table into context. Joe hadn't been signaling his daughter for some kind of collusion during the game. He'd simply been proud of her.

Chase's heart sank a little farther.

"I'm surprised she left you to wait out here alone," he observed, turning to peer in the direction he'd seen her wander. Eyes hungry for a sign of her.

"I wouldn't let her stay." Stuffing his hands in the pockets of the pantsuit jacket, Joe faced Chase again. "She washed her hands of my life even before she turned eighteen. And once that girl makes up her mind about something, she doesn't change it."

Chase felt like her father was beating the last of Chase's hopes to death. He rubbed his hand over his chest, wishing he were with Tana now. He needed to at least be sure she got home safely.

"Did you see if someone picked her up?" Chase withdrew his phone, ready to text one of her girlfriends.

"A couple of her theater friends were meeting her." Joe stopped, turning his head. The sound of a distant siren rode the breeze. "Look, my time is almost up, so I'm going to tell you what I told Tana. I've only got a year or so to live at most, so I realize the jail time I'm facing isn't adequate to pay my debt to you or society."

Alarm rattled through him. "What do you mean a year to live?"

But Joe shook his head as if he preferred not to answer. "Listen, Chase. I tried to send Tana a couple postcards with the coordinates on that land I left her, but she didn't realize what they meant. I buried some of my winnings there. Half is for her that I won fair and square off of blowhards like Carmichael. But the other half is money I owe to people I conned. It's all written down."

The words came fast even though Chase had a whole host of questions. But the sound of the sirens was growing closer.

"Are you saying you never took anyone's money?

That you buried it all?" Chase wondered if the guy had ever even left the country or if he'd been in disguises since going off the grid eight years ago.

"I took a little," he admitted, wincing as if he had a sudden pain in his side. But he straightened up again. "But it was never about the money for me. It was about the thrill. A game that hurt too many people."

"Like my mother," Chase reminded him bitterly. "I got back the lands, but I couldn't fix the way you hurt her."

"I will never forgive myself for hurting Margot. Regret for that—for what I did to her—is what got me into group therapy." He turned to face the public parking area as the police cars pulled in, headlights illuminating his face. "I really did want to leave the country with her. Tana's mother had already kicked me to the curb. But I couldn't let Margot tie herself to me."

In the swirl of blue and red lights, Chase could see how haggard the other man looked as he lifted his hands above his head.

Regret sighed through him for a hundred ways he'd screwed up tonight. For the first time ever, he felt the smallest twinge of empathy for Joe Blackstone. It wasn't a good feeling to know you'd messed up, possibly beyond repair, and hurt someone you cared about.

Because whether or not Joe had ever really cared for Chase's mom, Chase believed he cared for Tana. The grifter had proven it to him tonight by turning himself in. By the obvious pride he'd taken in watching her play. By the way he'd tried to make up for some of his wrongs.

Maybe that was why he found himself telling him, "For what it's worth, my mother forgave you a long time ago."

Chase wasn't sure he'd ever extend the same grace to the man. But he didn't mind giving him this small gift. It was true enough.

Two police officers neared them now. Chase prepared to explain who he was, but for now he held his hands in the air, too, just to be safe.

Joe Blackstone met his gaze in the moonlight. "Thank you for that. And good luck winning my girl back. She's hurt and she's angry. But she loved you eight years ago. If you're lucky and she still does, maybe you've got a shot."

Chase would gamble everything he had on the smallest chance the old man was right.

Walking home from another audition late the next Friday afternoon, Tana did not take her studded high-top tennis shoes for granted. They were comfortable for one thing, unlike last week's high heels.

And they'd been on her feet for her second callback for the soap opera. She hadn't gotten the bit part intended for a pretty face that she'd tried out for the week before. But the casting director had liked her reading and had asked her to try out for a new character on the show. A tough, streetwise woman raised by derelicts who triumphed over her past to open a bar in Port Henry, where the show was set. And the stars had aligned for the reading, apparently, because she got that part.

Yet even as Tana knew she should be on cloud nine over the professional victory, she felt more fragile than ever in the wake of Chase's accusation. A week apart hadn't soothed the burn of that wound in the least.

Of course, she shouldn't have been surprised that he didn't trust her. His request before the game that she not cheat showed her how much the past was still on his mind. How much he still viewed her as her father's daughter. It was like eight years of good behavior meant nothing.

Now, turning the corner in front of Fort Greene Park, she wondered if she even wanted to go home, where her roommates would doubtless want to celebrate her new role. Sable was moving out tomorrow for good, so she'd promised to sleep over one last time. No way would Tana miss out on that.

So why did she contemplate walking back to the park so she could cry in private on a park bench for a few hours? Her numbness cloak had worn off as soon as she'd left the Hamptons last weekend.

Instead of indulging the crying spree the way she wanted, she picked her head up as she reached her stoop.

Only to find Chase Serrano seated there. A black Stetson shaded his eyes, his denim-clad knees sprawled to either side of him.

Her heartbeat went into triple time while her brain counseled her to retreat. Fast.

But did tough, streetwise women run and hide at the first sign of trouble? She tried to think like her new character, bar owner Liberty Montgomery. For once, she was grateful for the chance to play the role of someone else around Chase.

"I think you have the wrong address," she informed him, fisting her hands on her hips. Willing her eyes not to fill with tears…or her heart to fill with hope. "Because I'm sure I told you we wouldn't be seeing each other again."

She wouldn't allow him to hurt her again. So her best defense was a good offense.

Except he didn't look offended. He looked like he hadn't slept either, the purple shadows under his eyes matching the ones she'd been seeing in the mirror all week on her own face.

"Tana, I'm so sorry." His words were quieter than she would have expected. Humble.

He spun something in his hands, worrying it back and forth in an agitated motion.

A sparkle from the object made her look closer. Her heart seized. It was the engagement ring she'd slammed into his palm at the party.

She told herself that even feisty Liberty Montgomery would have had her interest piqued. She looked at him levelly, grateful he was seated.

"For what exactly?" she asked.

An unhappy smile ghosted over his features. "How much time do you have?"

Around them, the street was quiet. There were a couple of teenage girls sharing a pair of earbuds, each engrossed in a phone screen. A package delivery carrier ran up to a house across the street.

She waited. "I'm listening."

His hands went still. "For taking for granted the time we had together. For using it to pursue a revenge scheme that didn't matter to me. For asking you to play that cursed game in the first place." He shook his head, gaze falling to the concrete steps briefly before meeting her eyes again. "But most of all? I regret letting my fears speak for me that night on the beach instead of listening to my gut and everything I knew about you."

The sadness etched in his features spoke to her as much as his words. Seeing that regret for herself softened something inside her. Made her want to hear more.

Taking a chance, she dismissed her Liberty character and ventured closer to Chase. She leaned a hip on the stone balustrade.

"You mean about accusing me of cheating?" Even now, a phantom pain came with the word. "You realize the dread of being associated with dishonesty is what drove me to cut ties with my dad in the first place, right? I didn't want that to taint the person I needed to become. But you insisted on seeing me that way."

"I didn't. I *don't* see you that way." He pivoted the ring back and forth, catching the light with the familiar stones. "If I'd used logic, Tana, I would have known the truth right away. You've shown me in a hundred ways that you're not the person I was afraid you were eight years ago. But I was scared of finding out I'd been deceived again, and I let my mouth run with the fears instead of listening."

She'd protected herself for so long, afraid of letting herself get too close to anyone, that she'd almost lost out on the chance to make the friends she had now. Friends who were—she could see out of the corner of her eye—sneaking peeks at them out the front window even now.

What if she took a chance with Chase, the same way she had with her girlfriends? It was easier with Blair and Sable. They'd lavished her with love so readily. But she knew that—if it worked—the payoff with Chase would be even greater. So she cracked open some of her pain, sharing it with him so he understood it.

"Whatever the cause, Chase, it hurt me so much to find out we were right back where we were at the beginning. As if the time we'd spent together meant nothing to you." She held herself very still, feeling vulnerable. Wary.

"I would do anything to undo that, Tana. Anything." His silver eyes were bright and flinty at the same time. Emotional, but determined. "But since I can't go back and change that night, I can lay the whole world at your feet and hope you try to forgive me."

Hope wound through her, even as she cautioned herself not to be wooed by words.

"What do you mean?" She didn't care about material things. But she couldn't deny she was curious. What woman wouldn't be at that kind of declaration?

"I'm asking you to spend time with me and let me show you how deeply I care about you. How much I love you." He juggled the ring to one hand and reached for hers with the other. "I've missed you for eight years. I didn't know how much until we spent time together again. But having you at my side in Cloverfield felt so right, I think I knew then that you're the only woman for me."

Her heart expanded. A deep breath filled her lungs in a way that made her think she hadn't really breathed for a whole week. It felt glorious. Happy. Hopeful.

"Chase." She couldn't think quite what else to say, so she just squeezed his strong hand, letting herself get lost in that molten silver stare and allowing the feeling of love to wrap her up. "It felt really right for me, too. When we were back at Cloverfield again." Then, as the words started to come, she found more. "I loved you from that first night we were together eight years ago," she admitted, letting go of her most closely guarded secret. "Don't let the clothes fool you. I might be more romantic than both my roommates combined."

A moment later, she was in Chase's strong arms, her head tucked against his chest and her hip tucked into his lap. He stroked her back with one broad palm and kissed the top of her hair with the other.

"Tana, I love you so much. I promise you're never going to regret being with me," he vowed before lifting her chin to look into her eyes. "You know the real reason I wanted you to be my pretend fiancée?"

In her peripheral vision, she saw the curtains at the front window flutter. But her attention remained on the pink diamonds that covered the engagement ring he held in front of her again.

"I kept asking you," she reminded him softly, biting her lip against the new surge of hopes that were wildly romantic. Foolish, even. "I never understood why we needed to pretend."

"I think the reason I could never come up with a very good answer is because I never wanted it to be fake." He stroked her hair off her temple, tucking it behind her ear. "I know you might not be ready to make that kind of commitment yet, but we could call it a promise ring—"

"As in you promise to propose one day?" She tried to imagine what life would be like with Chase Serrano in it every day.

A shiver ran over her at the idea of being in his arms. In his bed. But she also liked the idea of going horseback riding with him. Sharing her dreams with him. Filming him and their life together.

"That is absolutely what I'm promising. I just know I want you to have it back, whether you put it on your finger today or not."

Her heart leaped. She already knew her answer.

She leaned closer to kiss him, letting her lips glide over his slowly. Thoroughly.

This time, she could hear feminine squeals right through the front room window. She drew back on a laugh and saw that Chase's smile matched hers.

"I'm glad someone else is enjoying this, Tana, because facing you and knowing you had every reason to turn me down is the scariest thing I've ever done." Brandishing the ring once more, lifting it high enough that anyone in the peanut gallery would be able to see it, he held it above Tana's hand. "Would you like to wear it now?"

Joy filled her whole being. She couldn't remember ever feeling a smile so big. "I'd like to if you say the promise that goes with it."

His gaze went a shade darker as he stared into her eyes.

"Tana Blackstone, I promise you all my love and all my trust." The hand on her back rubbed lightly, as if he could make the words sink in with his touch. "And I also promise that when the time is right, and we've mapped out a life that will make you the happiest, I will ask you to be my wife."

Moisture gathered in the corners of her eyes. She didn't bother to blink it away, ready to let him see how much he affected her. How much she returned all those feelings.

"Yes, please, Chase Serrano. I love you. I forgive you. And I can't wait to say yes."

When the ring slid on her finger, Tana felt like her whole life slid into place. She had a job. A future with a man she loved. A happy final night with her girlfriends to celebrate her good fortune and theirs.

And most of all, she had a love she could count on forever.

Epilogue

One month later

Tana's finger hovered over the button on her phone that would almost empty her bank account. She made sure she had input the correct routing number for the money's destination.

Seated at a small dressing table in her room inside the Brooklyn brownstone, she had a few minutes to finish the financial transaction that would disperse the last of her father's gambling winnings. She'd been stunned when she and Chase had flown to Cloverfield to dig up the buried money and log book her father had kept from his poker heyday. Sure enough, there was a thorough accounting for two years' worth of his games and a list of everyone who'd lost money to him through trickery. Tana had a hard time finding a couple of the people on the list, but it had been rewarding labor to restore money to people who'd thought it had been lost for good.

Of course, there'd been a few players who'd still been angry with her father. But even the most bitter of Joe's victims had been appeased to hear he was serving time behind bars. One woman had even cried on the phone over the news and had sworn she would write to him.

"Are you sure about this?" Chase's low rumble from behind Tana preceded a kiss on the top of her head. He squeezed her shoulders, the scent of his aftershave making her long to lean back against him. "That's a lot of money you're giving away."

Refocusing on the numbers on her screen, Tana didn't need to think twice about the amount. The leftover funds in her father's buried lockbox had been fairly won, but that didn't mean she wanted any of it. Walking away from that life meant she had no intention of keeping a penny from his card sharp days. Besides, with the earnings from her regular work as an actress now that she had a steady role, finances were no longer an ever-present concern for Tana.

"Positive." She stabbed the send button with her finger and watched a confirmation number for the transaction appear on the screen. A sense of calm relief filled her to know the money had been given to a worthy cause. "I told my dad what I planned to do with the money and he really liked knowing it was supporting my friend's non-profit startup." Setting the device aside, she rose to her feet, turning so she could wind her arms around Chase's neck. "Now Blair can take her beauty program on the road in a customized cargo van that advertises her care services for cancer patients."

Tana and Sable had helped Blair launch the program when they saw how much time Blair devoted to offering free beauty services to people going through chemotherapy alongside her mother. Blair's mom had a hopeful prognosis now, but Blair continued to be passionate about the community of underserved people who were often too tired or discouraged for self-nurturing. Tana had been enthusiastic about the project from the beginning. And now, seeing her dad's decline in health due to pancreatic cancer, it felt all the more fitting to channel his winnings this way.

"Have I mentioned that I am so proud of who you are?" Chase asked, cupping her face in his hands as his gray eyes peered down into hers.

Happiness swelled inside her, the way it always seemed to when he was around. In the last four weeks, they'd found an easy rhythm to being together. He'd taken a suite at a hotel close to the Brooklyn pier where her performance of *A Streetcar Named Desire* had been, close enough to her brownstone that they could see each other daily. They'd spent two weekends at his house in Southampton so they could go horseback riding, but they talked about spending next summer at Cloverfield so they could ride every day. The nice thing about working on a soap opera was that she'd have a few months off before they began shooting again in the fall.

Maybe then she'd work on some ideas she had for producing. Now that her life had calmed down, she found herself reaching for her video camera more and more often.

When she wasn't reaching for Chase, at least.

"You may have mentioned it." She smiled up at him, mesmerized by the look in his eyes that told her how much he loved her. How much he trusted her. "But I don't think I'll ever get tired of hearing it."

She'd spent so long trying to recalibrate her ethics after her childhood that it still thrilled her to hear that Chase saw her in such a strongly positive light. His faith in her had her reaching for her spikes less and less often. But she still liked sketching the occasional monster on her wrists in henna. She'd done a dragon with lacy wings two nights ago and she'd toyed with the idea of turning him into a cartoon character. How fun would it be to create a kids' show for her first production?

"You're an amazing woman, Tana Blackstone." He spoke into her hairline as he kissed her, pressing the words into her skin for emphasis. "You inspire me to be a better person, and I can't believe I'm the fortunate one who gets to have you by my side."

She hummed something inarticulate in answer, her whole life vibrating along a new, happy chord. Pressing herself tighter against him, she let the feel of hard muscle and warm man tempt her to lead him toward her bed.

Until a shout sounded from downstairs.

"Tana, let's go!" Blair called from the next floor down. She and Lucas were moving in together soon, but they were taking their time to find the perfect place, and Tana had appreciated the bonus weeks with her friend. "You know Sable will strangle us if we're not on time for the courtroom vows!"

Chase leaned away from her, chuckling softly as his hold on her eased. "Guess we'd better get going."

"Right." Tana retrieved her phone and a small, beaded bag for the low-key nuptials that would tie Sable to Roman, her baby's father, until after their child's birth. There would be a beach wedding next summer, but the two of them wanted to make their marriage official today. Tana was honored to have been asked. Blair and Lucas would join Tana and Chase to witness the event before a catered dinner at the brownstone for old times' sake. "Never keep a pregnant woman waiting."

Chase kept one of her hands in his and he tugged on it briefly as they reached the top of the staircase.

"I can't wait until it's our turn." He lifted her ring finger to her lips and kissed the spot just above her engagement diamond.

Her pulse sped, the way it always did when he was near. Especially when he said things like that.

"I bet it will happen sooner than you think, if you play your cards right." With a wink, she brushed past him to head down the stairs, more than ready to celebrate happily-ever-afters with the people she loved most in the world.

* * * * *

"What do you want to ask me, Sloan?"

He drew in a deep breath. "I need to know what made you come looking for me last night."

She broke eye contact with him and glanced out the window, not saying anything for a moment. "You were gone longer than you said you would be. I got worried. It was either go see what was taking you so long or pace the floor with worry even more. I chose the former."

"But the weather had turned into a blizzard, Les." He then realized he'd called her what he'd normally called her while they'd been together. She had been Les and not Leslie.

"I know that. I also knew you were out there in it. I tried to convince myself that you could take care of yourself, but I also knew with the amount of wind blowing and snow coming down that anything could have happened."

She paused again before saying, "Chances are, you would have made it back to the cabin, but I couldn't risk the chance you would not have."

He tried not to concentrate on the sadness he heard in her voice and saw in her eyes. Instead, he concentrated on her mouth and in doing so was reminded of just how it tasted. "Not sure if I would have made it back, Les. My head was hurting, and it was getting harder and harder to make my body move because I was so cold. Hell, I wasn't even sure I was going in the right direction. I regret you put your own life at risk, but I'm damn glad you were there when I needed you."

"Just like you were there for me and my company when I needed you, Sloan," she said softly.

Her words made him realize that they'd been there for each other when it had mattered the most. He didn't want to think what would have been the outcome if he'd been at the cabin alone as originally planned and the snowstorm hit. Nor did he want to think what would have happened to her and her company if Redford hadn't told him what was going on. The potential outcome of either made him shiver.

"You're still cold. I'd better go and get that hot chocolate going," she said, shifting to get up and reach for her clothes.

"Don't go yet," he said, not ready for any distance to be put between them or their bodies.

She glanced over at him. Their gazes held and then, as if she'd just noticed his erection pressing against her thigh, she said, "You do know the only reason why we're naked in this sleeping bag together, right?"

He nodded. "Yes. Because I needed your body's heat last night." He inched his mouth closer to hers and then said, "Only problem is, I still need your body's heat, Les. But now I need it for a totally different reason."

And then he leaned in and kissed her.

Don't miss what happens next in...
What He Wants for Christmas *by Brenda Jackson,*
the next book in her Westmoreland Legacy:
The Outlaws series!

Available December 2021 wherever
Harlequin Desire books and ebooks are sold.

Harlequin.com

HDEXP1121

Love Harlequin romance?

DISCOVER.

Be the first to find out about promotions, news and exclusive content!

Facebook.com/HarlequinBooks

Twitter.com/HarlequinBooks

Instagram.com/HarlequinBooks

Pinterest.com/HarlequinBooks

YouTube.com/HarlequinBooks

ReaderService.com

EXPLORE.

Sign up for the Harlequin e-newsletter and download a free book from any series at
TryHarlequin.com

CONNECT.

Join our Harlequin community to share your thoughts and connect with other romance readers!
Facebook.com/groups/HarlequinConnection

HARLEQUIN

Heartfelt or thrilling, passionate or uplifting—Harlequin is more than just happily-ever-after.

With twelve different series to choose from and new books available every month, you are sure to find stories that will move you, uplift you, inspire and delight you.

SIGN UP FOR THE HARLEQUIN NEWSLETTER

Be the first to hear about great new reads and exciting offers!

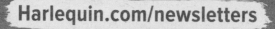

Harlequin.com/newsletters